Tak

TAKING THE HIGH ROAD

Meet Kilfinan and its improbable saints

Harry Hunter

First published in 2014
by Highland Books Ltd, 2 High Pines, Knoll
Road, Godalming, Surrey, GU7 2EP

Cover picture by Brian Murray.

ISBN-10 1-897913-91-5
ISBN-13 978-1897913-91-8

ebook ISBN-13 978-1909690-91-2

Contents

Preface

A couple of years back, I was struck by a report which showed that the biggest single reason for people leaving the church was its perceived irrelevance to their daily lives. Sunday mornings were a rarefied retreat from the realities of the working week. Mark Greene's *Thank God It's Monday* was a welcome attempt to show how practical Christianity can meet the needs of people in their everyday situations, as well as appeal to those who are un-churched and de-churched.

This collection of short stories tells of the trials and tribulations of Sam and Penny Waite. They are an active church couple whose plan is to commit to a 'churchier' role, but discover that a more powerful ministry actually lies in the daily reality of people's life and work.

From their well-established home and careers in 'middle England', they suddenly find themselves displaced to the West Coast of Scotland at the height of the independence debate. This unexpected jolt helps them discover more about themselves and about what God might have in mind for them.

These stories have been written in *Highland Books'* tradition of 'pick-me-ups'. Each chapter is a self-contained short story, although each contributes to an over-arching tale. You may find that the stories make more sense when read in sequence though, hopefully, they also make sense when picked up at random.

I must give particular thanks to two people for helping me write this collection. The first is my wife, Jill, who has been simultaneously my most constructive and most fearless critic, as well as my constant encourager. The second is Philip Ralli, Editorial Director of Highland Books, who urged me to find a 'voice' for my narrator and thereby caused me to stumble across the Waites and Kilfinan.

I hope that you can pick up this book for quarter of an hour, and put it down having finished a particular story. I hope that you will also find the stories are spiritual pick-me-ups, and that you will be able to identify with the problems, hopes and occasional triumphs of the folk of Kilfinan.

Harry Hunter

1. LLOYD:

An Unwelcome Companion

Late one morning in summer 2010 I recalled why I rarely travelled by train. On the few occasions when I did, it was first class, claimed on expenses. Today I had been advised against bringing my car into the centre of Lincoln. Having to pay the rail fare myself, I risked standard class for the first time in a decade.

The carriage was rather too warm and crowded, but nothing that couldn't be tolerated for an hour. We had set off reassuringly promptly and the journey had been sufficiently peaceful for me to mentally rehearse the questions for my impending interview. I was to be screened for training as a lay reader in the Church of England and, as a structural engineer by *métier,* verbal dexterity wasn't always my strong point. Numeracy came naturally to me; improvised ripostes to tricky theological points didn't. But by the time we pulled into our first stop I was reasonably confident of dealing with any questions that the panel might lob at me. Resting my head against the unnecessarily firm upholstery, I slowly cleared my mind of distractions.

The train started to fill up alarmingly and I was resigned to losing the empty seat facing me. A lanky man, early thirties at a guess and decked in a garish Argyle pullover which jarred with his crumpled brown slacks, smiled at me enthusiastically and asked "Is this seat taken?"

I gestured that he was free to occupy it. As he did so, he continued to fix me with the gaze of an over-excited puppy.

I shut my eyes and conjectured impressive responses to the questions the panel might throw at me. I was aware it would include a fashionably liberal suffragan bishop, so I sought to locate my answers in a non-contentious territory that would accommodate his postmodern tastes without compromising my rather old-fashioned evangelical beliefs. I supposed this was the kind of mental sparring they would appreciate.

Just then I heard a voice:

"Nice daydream, guv?"

It took a moment for the words to filter through, but I was aware that the other two passengers at our table were women, and the speaker would hardly address them as "guv". I opened my eyes and saw puppy-man staring at me. His gambit struck me as impertinent, and I was inclined to silence him in a way that would put an end to his over-familiarity for the remainder of the journey.

But quick thinking isn't my strong point and I fumbled for a withering put-down. At work, I had several colleagues who were dazzlingly spontaneous and who could have responded with the *mot juste*, but I was old Sam Waite who always thought of the *mot d'escalier*. I would stumble upon the perfect response a moment too late to have the desired effect. Little wonder they called me *Old Sam Makeweight*. It was in jest, of course – they respected my ability and loyalty – but my flatfootedness had become a trade-mark.

"You looked like you were miles away," he said with an anticipatory grin. I resented the over-familiarity, but could see that the ladies on the window seat were tuning in with amusement despite their feigned insouciance.

"I was thinking," I replied, not able to come up with a pithier response, but with an irascible tone that indicated I'd prefer to continue the journey in silence.

"Must've been important. You looked like some Greek philosopher. By the way, it's Lloyd."

"Sam," I muttered grudgingly in return. "Actually, I've got an interview," I added, immediately regretting my unnecessary admission. He seized on it with glee.

"Oooh, exciting. New job, eh. Pays well, does it?"

I was about to bark at him to mind his own business, but an inner voice nagged me that I was Christ's ambassador; besides, the two ladies had involuntary pricked up an ear, whilst pretending to read their novels.

"Actually it's just a voluntary post. I already have a job that I'm perfectly happy with," I said as dismissively as possible, hopeful that this would deter any further intrusions.

But he was not to be derailed. "Do-gooder, then are we? Wanting to do our bit for Big Society?", he intoned with mock irony.

Only my innate sense of Christian charity prevented me from blanking him.

"No it's not that kind of volunteering. It just happens to be an unpaid role."

"Too much time on your hands, eh? On your own, are you?"

Lloyd's persistence was insufferable. He looked unkempt and disorganised. I was glad to be sitting across from, rather than next to, him because I suspected he probably smelt. I was on the point of losing my composure and telling him to mind his own business, but instead settled for a carefully judged tone of irritation.

"I'm happily married, with two children, and have a demanding job in industry." As I buried my head in my paper, he desisted for all of ten seconds.

"What does your wife think of it, then?"

I pretended not to hear but he continued, "You working all those extra hours instead of being at home?"

From his childishly mischievous expression I could tell he was trying to stir up trouble. Actually he had a point, though I could hardly admit it. Penny wasn't best pleased about the amount of training that was involved in becoming a lay reader. She felt it was another excuse to avoid spending time with her or making myself useful around the house.

We had only reached some sort of domestic truce because I agreed that it would be her turn next. She was very keen to undertake ministerial training, but had reluctantly conceded that she needed a couple more years to concentrate on a business career before embarking on major new church commitments. And indeed, she had been encouraged by the bishop to consider full ordination rather than just lay reader training, as he reckoned she had the ability to 'go all the way'. The Church of England was finally inching forward on women bishops, and the senior hierarchy were talent-spotting potential future candidates. Penny, I had little doubt, checked all the boxes you could wish for in relation to the episcopate.

"She's quite happy," I replied somewhat unconvincingly. "She's got her own interests, too".

"I'll believe you. Thousands wouldn't," he said sporting a perceptive grin. "What is it you do then?"

"I'm a structural engineer. I work on construction management of big projects," I replied, assuming that would be sufficiently technical and impressive to silence him.

"No. I mean, your volunteer stuff."

I was afraid that that was what he'd meant. Somehow, I was embarrassed to talk about it publicly, especially as we were attracting a growing radius of earwiggers. I composed myself, so that my annoyance wouldn't be too obvious. Taking a deep breath, I told him, "I help to lead church services. I'm about to be interviewed for lay reader training."

This drew a puzzled but inquisitive look. I continued before he could ask the obvious question. "It's a bit like being a vicar, but unpaid."

A thin silence settled on our surrounding passengers and I rather wished the train would pull into a station and let them alight, but the next stop was a good twenty minutes.

After a few moments he interjected, "You work among engineers then? Surely those techie people don't believe in God? What do you do say to them? I bet you don't let on about it at work, do you?"

He was touching on a very sensitive and personal issue. I convinced myself it was none of his business. My mind raced for evidence that I did actually share my faith with colleagues.

"Actually you'd be surprised. I have colleagues who do talk to me about private issues. What you might call spiritual issues. It happens more often than you might think." It was, to be honest, an exaggeration, even a fib. My mind raced frantically and somehow I managed to dredge up a couple of illustrations where faith and business had loosely coincided.

Fortunately, though, his eyes suggested a butterfly mind that was already flitting to another line of questioning.

"Don't care for religion, myself," he ventured at length.

"Really."

"No. Jesus was okay, I mean. Can't see much wrong with him. But I don't have time for the church."

"It's a complex issue," I muttered in a fatuous sort of way.

He stared at me for a moment, clearly bent on protracting a one-sided conversation for as long as possible. I couldn't be bothered with his irksome manner, although it was evidently his customary practice.

"What's your problem with the church?", I asked. I was starting to gain a little confidence. Asking him a question at least put me on the front foot for a change.

It was his turn to feel discomfited. "Well, I mean," he started at length, "Jesus was a decent enough bloke, okay. He went around being a generally good guy and telling us how to be better people. And then the church comes along and starts torturing people and going to war and oppressing women…"

His voice was rising. By now, half the carriage was looking at us. From choice, I would have answered him with an indignant harrumph but we were now too public for me to retreat gracefully.

I had to produce a convincing answer, quickly. "But think of all the good," I replied. "Think of the Christians who built hospitals, schools, abolished slavery. They didn't do it just because they were do-gooders, they did it because Jesus commanded them to do these things for the least of His brothers and sisters. They changed history."

I had scored my first, very palpable, hit.

Lloyd was momentarily lost for an answer. He looked at me quizzically and something like a smile began to suffuse across his face. At last, I had shut him up, or so I thought. But I was mistaken.

"Okay, so what about all the child abuse? Over 3000 priests were in on that game. What have you got to say about that?" I detected a murmur of agreement from our growing audience.

"Out of over 400,000 priests, I believe." Thank goodness I'd read a recent report. "Of course," I conceded, "there'll always be some bad 'uns in any organisation. But look at all the excellent priests working tirelessly around the world. Sacrificially, I would say."

Touché. I felt my response was rather good, and I heard no noises of dissent. But it still didn't silence my interrogator.

"Fair point, guv. But why do you have to go to church and listen to all that mumbo jumbo. And sing all those miserable hymns?"

"When did you last actually go to church?", I quipped, this time without hesitation.

I was hoping for an admission that he hadn't actually darkened the door of a church in decades and was out of touch with modern worship, but something had clearly caught his eye. Instead of harassing me with more questions, he gazed past my shoulder with the haunted look of a malnourished child. His mouth quivered and actually salivated. Looking at him again, I did detect a rather gaunt frame beneath his scarecrow clothes.

From the corner of my eye I spotted the gradual approach of the catering trolley. My interlocutor's hungered expression made me realise that it was now after midday and I was getting peckish. I helped myself to a cheese and pickle sandwich, a biscuit and a mineral water and proffered a tenner.

But before the trolleyman could accept it I heard, "That looks good, guv."

The tone of Lloyd's voice had turned from impertinent to beseeching. "I haven't had a bite to eat yet today." This personal plea was executed in such a way as to pierce the near-silence of the carriage. It drew a stifled titter.

I stared back at him with a tight-lipped expression. "Very well, then."

And with, "Aah, you're a star, guv", he helped himself to a similar lunch, but with more expensive variants. The trolleyman lowered his eyes dubiously at my tenner. I put it away and replaced it with a £20 note, which received depressingly little change in return.

The lunch at least silenced him, apart from occasional grunts of "aw, that's tasty" and, "cor, I could go another of those". Faces all around the carriage turned to glance in my direction and I felt that 'mug' must have been written prominently across my face.

As he drained the final drop of his drink he seemed to gain a second wind. But he had barely resumed his cross-examination when the train started to slow and he craned his neck sharply. "Oi, it's my station. Nearly missed it, eh. Almost ended up going all the way to Lincoln with you. Good talking to you guv. Hope the interview goes well."

I smiled at him in relief. As he was leaving his seat, for some reason I decided to give him a tract.

It's not something I would normally do, unless I had just finished an intensely private conversation with someone who wanted to explore the faith further. Perhaps I thought he would just look at it supercili- ously and stick it quietly in a pocket.

But instead, he announced it to the whole carriage. "Eh, look at that. *How to Become a Christian*. 'Ere you don't miss a trick do you, Reverend? Anyone want a copy?"

I prayed that the ground would swallow me up. Many eyes and smirking lips turned in my direction. The rest of the journey seemed an eternity, but it wasn't a second longer than it should have been and the train eventually drew into Lincoln with almost Swiss punctuality. I felt my ears burning and tried to appear as calm as possible as I buffeted my way off the carriage and towards the taxi stand.

Arriving at the Minster Walk I instantly felt in my comfort zone. Here was a safe place. Tranquil and cloistered. Here were people who would treat me graciously and speak my language. However, the interlude with Lloyd had at least served the purpose of distracting me from the interview. As I followed the signs to the appointed room I was sufficiently nervous to realise that my journey might have other- wise been a fretful one.

I was invited into an ante-room by a strikingly young and charming secretary who instantly put me at ease, and shortly after asked me to proceed to the interview room, where I was confronted by a panel comprising the suffragan, a man and a woman wearing dog collars, and another early-middle-aged woman who announced herself as a recently licensed lay reader.

After half a minute of affable smiles and introductions, the suffragan kicked off with a question about the extent to which I'd discussed the application with my wife and how she viewed the prospect of my three year commitment to training. He glanced down at his notes and a glint came to his eye. "Is she really a *pennyweight*?", he quipped, breaking into a prolonged chuckle and conveying immense satisfaction at his witticism.

I groaned internally and, had it been other than the suffragan bishop himself, might have been none too polite about people who think they are the first to have spotted the wearisome pun. It was Penny's principal misgiving when I proposed to her and has been a source of irritation ever since.

However, I forced myself to feign a smile, whilst at the same time mentally retrieving the response that I had previously given to Lloyd. I found myself able to reply rather compellingly about how we both felt we were being called to serve God more fully, but our respective stages of career meant that I should make the first move. In due course, I would give her my unqualified support to take her own ministry forward, which would be distinctively different from mine. The panel nodded approvingly.

Then they asked about my particular sense of vocation to ministry and mission, and the ways in which this had been confirmed by others. They asked me about my witness as a Christian at work. Fortuitously, I could produce a couple of convincing anecdotes without hesitation. Without Lloyd's previous spur, I should certainly have been at a total loss.

As the interview drew to a close, the suffragan asked with a winsome smile, "Now, Sam, suppose you are in a very public place and you have the opportunity to witness. How would you feel about it?"

Until a couple of hours ago, the question would have floored me, and I wouldn't have been able to fabricate even a hypothetical example. But – being as vague as possible about the date and circumstances – I was able to commence, "Well, it's funny you should say that, but…".

My vivid and compelling reply clearly caused great amusement, as well as many hums of approval and cringes of vicarious embarrassment.

Finally, the lady wearing a dog collar was invited to lob in a 'wildcard' question. She thought for a moment, then asked whether I believed in angels. What did the writer of the letter to the Hebrews mean, for example, when he spoke of entertaining angels unawares?

Within a second, I felt a glow of realisation suffuse across me. I smiled knowingly. "I think it's exceptionally likely that angels are walking amongst us all the time." I pondered for a moment. "Perhaps, it's most important that you show hospitality, even to people whose company you don't particularly enjoy. If you have the chance, buy them lunch."

I think it was the twinkle in my eye that convinced them. For once, *Old Makeweight* wasn't left to rue the *mot d'escalier*. He had given the *mot juste*.

And so it was that, with a little unexpected help from Lloyd, I embarked on my training and three years later saw my name go up on the church notice board as Lay Reader, with Penny waiting in the wings to follow her own calling.

But God had other plans for us.

2. MAX:
Too Good
To Be True?

It was August 2013, less than three months since my boss had unexpectedly summoned me to his office. I recalled how I'd steeled myself for a carpeting, though had no idea of how I might have erred. In truth, he rarely needed a good reason to tear a strip off some undeserving sap, and seemed at times to select a scapegoat at random *pour encourager les autres*. I had rapped on his door with *faux* confidence and awaited his trademark command to enter. So, I was much relieved when he smiled and gestured winsomely towards the expensively upholstered seats in the 'creative' corner of his room.

The reason for my summons quickly became clear. My annual performance review had confirmed that I was worthy of a promotion, and a perfect opportunity had arisen. He flattered me to the point where my agreement was practically a formality, and described how the range of responsibilities would be right up my street.

"There's one minor issue, though, Sam," he added in a nonchalant voice, almost as an afterthought. "It's at our Kilfinan office, on the West Coast of Scotland. Are you familiar with it?"

I froze. "No, no, not really. Well, vaguely. Isn't there a depot or something?", I stammered, trying to conceal my shock. In all my life, I had never been, nor desired to venture, further north than York.

"Used to be a depot," he continued, with a high octane grin. "Being upgraded to a regional head-quarters. You'll like it."

My expression must have conveyed scepticism, even terror.

"Talk it over with Penelope. I'll give you a couple of days."

Suppressing a gulp, I thanked him as profusely and cheerfully as conscience would allow.

The fallout from that meeting can only be likened to our experience, ten years previously, when we had taken our children to a well known theme park and ridden on a legendary rollercoaster. By the time we reached the finish we had been rotated and disorientated until body, soul and spirit were centrifuged into their constituent elements. That was how we felt by the time we arrived at Kilfinan.

I should perhaps have paid more attention to Lloyd, an irritating chap who buttonholed me on the train three years previously. I recalled how he inquired about my wife's views on my readership training. With hindsight, it wouldn't have been a bad idea to have discussed it more fully with Penny, rather than consulting her after my own mind was pretty much made up. It might well have avoided arguments later on.

And, once my training had successfully concluded, it wouldn't have been a bad idea to have discussed more fully with her the prospect of a new job and its associated wrench from our Lincolnshire home of more than twenty years. Actually, I thought I'd broken the idea to her rather sensitively but that evidently wasn't her perception.

With hindsight, I realise I did rather pose it as a *fait accompli* and hadn't really solicited her opinion or prayed over the matter with as much candour as desirable. I really should have given more thought to her own aspirations because we'd absolutely agreed that as soon as I'd completed my training it would be her turn next. Her application to enter theological college and study for the priesthood was well advanced. But then, if I wanted to be self-justifying, I hadn't exactly been given much time to ponder my future options either.

Yet on reflection, I could see that my promotion was merely the ring-pull that opened a can of worms.

Anyway, I'll cut to the chase because you'll hear all the detail later on. Suffice to say, Penny nearly walked out on me – or, perhaps, it would have been more a case of her staying put and me moving up north by myself. Fortunately, we both stepped back from the brink and somehow, less than three months later, we had patched up our differences, found a rather delightful new house, worked our respective notices, crated our belongings and headed three hundred miles north-west to Kilfinan.

One of the things that made it a little easier was that Penny had just reached a juncture in her work where she'd gained sufficient experience and seniority to be able to branch out as a freelance. This was always her game plan in the event of training for the ministry, and events merely precipitated matters. She had also been encouraged about the opportunities that might beckon in the Episcopal church in Scotland.

One thing that made it more difficult, though, was the profound and barely concealed dismay among our clergy and friends at St John's, who had given me so much support in becoming a Lay Reader; no sooner had my name been painted on the church notice board, than I was announcing my departure. Our local ministry team was badly under-resourced. At least until that point they had been able to rely on the pair of us to contribute in one way or another to the church's various rotas, and my licensing had been anticipated with great optimism.

Anyway, whatever our tribulations by the time we finally reached our new home in Kilfinan, Penny's rapture at the sea view on our first morning gave us a welcome psychological and spiritual boost. I had been accorded a miserly two days house-moving leave, so it was a matter of hitting the ground running in terms of accustoming myself to my new colleagues and to the greatly increased responsibilities of my new role.

I had hoped in vain that my moniker of *Old Makeweight* would have stayed behind in Lincolnshire, but evidently the office grapevine ensured that my reputation preceded me and it was already in circulation during the first week. At least Penny could escape the irritation of being a *Pennyweight*, the progressively unfunny handle which had dogged her at work and church.

As a Lay Reader, I should have made it a priority to meet with the local Episcopal priest and offer my services. Initially I had been fired by curiosity about the local church scene; about the character and catchment of the 'piskies'; about the alternatives to the Episcopal church that might be available locally; about the training and career possibilities that might be open to Penny. As an afterthought, I had even wondered what God might have in mind for me.

But more urgent matters had intervened. There was little enough time to tidy up my files, brief my successor, get the house into a saleable condition, find a new place to live, get up to speed with my new role – and, above all, spend some quality time with Penny to heal a number of wounds. As a consequence, I had made no progress beyond making a virtual visit, via its website, to a local Episcopal church called St Finnan's.

Thus it was that we arrived entirely ill-prepared that first Sunday morning for the 10.30 service and were pleasantly surprised to discover a recently refurbished church interior with comfortable chairs in which we could locate ourselves inconspicuously.

It wasn't a bad service. A brief but workmanlike sermon from an affable priest called Max, competent singing, only minor traps for the uninitiated in the liturgy, surprisingly imaginative prayers from a Lay Reader called Ellie, and a promising level of eye contact as we shared the peace. We braced ourselves for the initial meeting with the Reverend Max Maxwell as we departed.

Mingling over coffee at the end of the service, we were generally encouraged by the number of people who noticed us as newcomers and enthusiastically ushered us in the right direction for refreshments and social groupings. We could see Max eying us from a distance. But it was Ellie who shortly descended on us from the wings.

'Descended' is perhaps an unfair term. It suggests she was an over-zealous predator waiting to pounce from her lair, but in reality her intervention was as gracious a welcome as anyone could have desired. I saw Penny flinch a little – and hoped that I hadn't done likewise – as this plain, greying slip of a woman with a rather prim voice introduced herself. Penny's first impression was that of the churchy sort of spinster whom she can only tolerate in minuscule doses.

However, first impressions are often misleading, and Christians should be wary of placing undue reliance on them. Ellie soon began to strike us as a contented and clear-thinking person, utterly dedicated to St Finnan's and its fellowship, and immediately recognising us as newcomers who needed to be welcomed without being overwhelmed. She had an entirely natural and engaging way of finding out about us, and of commending St Finnan's and all that it had to offer.

Before too long, we had spilled the beans about my recent licensing and Penny's ordination aspirations. To her credit, Ellie retained a measure of composure, despite her eyes betraying incredulity followed by glee.

"Then I must introduce you to Max", she said. "Look, he's free now." She caught Max's eye and beckoned him across to us.

As Ellie explained the situation to him, Max was barely able to conceal his amazement. Again, I'll tell you more in due course, but suffice to say that he insisted we visit him at the rectory a couple of days later.

As he left us, Ellie confided that she had been concerned about Max. He was woefully over-stretched and his health was suffering. She was troubled about his wellbeing and faith. Doubtless she wouldn't have admitted as much to any other newcomer, but she wasn't going to miss the opportunity to place the church's urgent need on our consciences. To her credit, she stopped just short of moral blackmail.

That Tuesday evening, we had the most positive of meetings with Max and were quickly inducted into the church's various rotas. With almost indecent haste, I was added to the rota for officiating at services whilst Penny, caught off guard, uncharacteristically agreed to being interim prayer secretary. That's a story in itself, which I'll leave for her to tell.

We left the rectory with a feeling that, if only we had spent more time in prayer regarding our relocation, we would have been better prepared to consider the St Finnan's option. Of course, there must have been several other churches which we should have checked out first. However, in our haste, we just had to trust that God had parachuted us into pre-moulded slots.

The next few weeks were a blur as I struggled to get on top of my new job and Penny set herself up as a sole trader and explored ministerial training options. So, it was almost Advent when Ellie took us aside after a team meeting.

She started off with an innocuous chat about how we were settling in and whether we were adjusting to the long wintry nights. Then, having judged that we were suitably warmed up, asked, "How do you find Max?"

Penny and I looked at each other. Ellie hadn't seemed the sort to encourage gossip.

"Fine," Penny smiled. "Friendly. Runs a tight ship. Seems to have good ideas. Why do you ask?"

I echoed her comments with a raising of my eyebrows. "Almost too good to be true," I added.

"Yes, he seems fine, doesn't he? But…," Ellie began.

"But…?" I interjected.

"But, I'm concerned. I wouldn't have mentioned it to anyone else. I'm sure he's suffering from too much stress. I know it's an over-used term these days, but there's no other way to describe it. It's taking a toll on his personal life and health. I'm worried that we should be doing something more."

"You mean he's trying to do way too much? A clergyman trying to do the work of three people. Tell me about it," Penny ventured in her business voice.

"Exactly. But that's just the half of it. He's become increasingly convinced that he's failing; that numbers and everything are down – that he's just not up to the job. He rarely says anything directly and he's always trying to keep everyone's spirits up, but occasionally he sinks into a depression. He never used to."

"I can't say I'd really noticed," I replied. "He always seems buzzy and purposeful. His sermons are upbeat. The church seems to be doing rather well."

Penny nodded in agreement. But Ellie was not to be de-railed from her train of thought.

"Yes, that's part of the problem. Max is terrific. Quite the best priest I've worked with. But I think he's slipping into a downward spiral. I don't know if you realise it, but you arrived just in time. He hasn't had a decent break in ages. He thinks that St Finnan's is going downhill and it's all his fault."

"And is it?"

"Not at all. But, you know, when you're so close, you can't step back and take a balanced view."

We both signalled our heartfelt recognition of the situation.

"Look, Ellie," suggested Penny as people started to depart for home, "why not join us for supper tomorrow and we can talk some more. It's about time we did."

Thus it was that we got to know Ellie better, and to bring ourselves up to speed on the history of St Finnan's.

Two things in particular stuck in my mind about our chat with Ellie, apart from what a surprisingly pleasant and quick-witted person she was. First, was her total lack of malice and judgementalism, always seeing the best in people. Second was the utter familiarity and predictability of the pressures that she recounted about Max.

We had feared that an evening with Ellie would be tiresome but actually it flew by. It was also remarkably conclusive. Although we seemed to chat about everything under the sun, we also agreed to fathom what exactly was happening at St Finnan's and also to work out how to ensure that Max got a decent break.

Fortunately, Penny and I had spent long enough in business to know how to research what was going on in organisations. We knew how easy it was for a manager to have a sense of failure when actually their business was faring well or, alternatively, to be bullish when it was teetering on the brink of bankruptcy. We were both adept at providing a reality check: analysing situations coolly and rationally to get a handle on the underlying situation. Without even needing to confer with each other, we began suggesting some practical measures to Ellie. Following her enthusiastic response, we announced to the congregation that they might receive some requests for information from us. Just in our capacity as newcomers, you understand, so we could take an impartial appraisal of the current state of play.

Over the following fortnight we trawled through various records of church meetings, interviewed a sample of the congregation and obtained a remarkably high response rate to a brief questionnaire we devised. Our report was eagerly awaited at the next vestry meeting.

Amazingly, it was the first time that Penny and I had shared a platform, and I think we both impressed each other with the snappiness and humour of our presentations.

I kicked off with a preamble about how St Finnan's appeared to be going through a tough phase, though our analysis revealed a somewhat different picture.

Max and several others looked sceptical.

Penny followed with a résumé of overall attendance and membership. She'd gone back through five years-worth of membership lists and major festival headcounts. The graphs were confusing at first glance but she demystified them with a series of amusingly illustrated slides. Although there were dips, these reflected occasions when outdated records were tidied up. Of course, rolls always became inflated by people who had actually left the area, or had been nominal members, or had remained active Christians but moved to a different church. However, when you synthesised all the evidence from attendance and membership, it was possible to discern a small increase. Only an extra six net attenders over the past four years, but at least it was a small increase rather than a small decrease. And when you tracked the congregation's age-sex pyramid over time, the demographic had actually become slightly more balanced.

The expressions of our audience were perky, if a little bemused.

I then reviewed the findings of our questionnaires and interviews. Whereas the ministry team had worried that modern styles of worship were encountering criticism, actually over eighty percent of the congregation supported the changes in hymnody and liturgy, and almost no-one had expressed a strong aversion.

It was clear, too, that sub-groups within the church were holding steady. Child and teenage groups had a strong core, with numbers swollen by special events. Leaders were a strongly committed bunch and were present in sufficient numbers to permit a degree of rotation. There was incipient concern about lack of sabbaticals amongst leaders and, whilst this was something that would need to be addressed, it was nothing unusual and there was no immediate urgency. House groups were a relatively recent innovation and remained quite small, but their fluctuations in numbers were consistent with people moving in and out of the area; all the leaders seemed optimistic that the groups were developing fellowship and deepening faith. Although there were only three small groups, it needed to be borne in mind that five years ago there were none at all.

Penny followed with an analysis of St Finnan's involvement in the wider community, in particular focusing on our role in the town's *Churches Together* organisation. Here perhaps there was a hint of a scattergun approach and a need for greater focus. Might it be that the churches were being over-ambitious and spreading themselves too thinly? Whilst there was clear evidence of the success and viability of its carers' support network, perhaps its other activities needed to be re-evaluated.

After fifteen minutes of quick-fire presentations, I rounded off with an upbeat summary pointing out that behind the apparent stagnation and perceived decline, the church was actually showing some very positive trends. It proved the value of taking a fresh look at a situation through outsiders' eyes.

"It's too easy," I concluded, "for the Devil to trick us into thinking we're losing ground and that we're riven with internal strife, when in fact we're doing rather well. There's no doubt that St Finnan's is in good underlying health and that its people are succeeding, little by little, in advancing Kingdom values."

We didn't quite know what to expect. We'd feared a backlash against our business-speak.

But in fact there was a subdued hush, as people assimilated what they'd heard. The silence was shortly broken by a growing crescendo of appreciation. Max actually appeared to relax, settling back into his chair with a smile.

We proceeded to have the most encouraging and productive of discussions which consumed considerably more time than our original presentation.

"But we have one more thing to add," Penny began. "It's absolutely imperative that Max gets a proper break. He must get a holiday and that long overdue sabbatical."

Despite a rousing chorus of "hear, hear!" and a ripple of applause, Max waved his hand and protested that no such thing was possible. Everyone was far too hard-pressed and, besides, simply hearing our report had given him new energy and purpose.

But we had out-manoeuvred him. Ellie had worked like a Trojan to extract support from elsewhere in the Diocese to cover for a decent absence.

Penny and I had surreptitiously collected money from the congregation, kick-started by a not inconsiderable contribution of our own, to defray the cost of a family holiday.

"Max, you need to get away," I insisted. We showed him a rota which would come into play from the following month, from which his name was conspicuously absent. The sabbatical was only semi-official, but there was a tacit agreement from higher echelons that he wouldn't be disturbed. Somehow, Ellie had devised it so that every service at every church in our shared benefice was covered, and every meeting chaired, for a two month period. I then presented him with an envelope containing sufficient funds for a couple of weeks in the sun. He was overwhelmed and almost unable to speak, but we gave him no option.

A two month respite was the very least he deserved. At one time he would have had twelve months.

All in all, we beat the Author of Lies at his own game, which always gives one a great deal of satisfaction. At least temporarily, we had used the methods of mammon the achieve the ends of God. And, by the time Lent arrived, we had a revitalised priest with a clear and positive vision about where his church was heading.

Inevitably, Ellie still regularly had to rein him back and remind him that if he didn't spend enough time in prayer and recuperation, he would relapse. Max, like all of us, needs to discover Ellie's gift for standing back peacefully, and looking in just the right places to see the inexorable advance of Kingdom values.

Yet when, a few months later, I chatted with Ellie about Max's rejuvenation she was less celebratory than I'd expected. Wasn't she unduly timorous, I cajoled? She looked at me pensively, then said:

"Yes, it's a wonderful thing that has happened. But things never turn out the way we expect. God has unforeseeable plans for us. And the Evil One is always scheming, too. We've won a battle, but the war goes on."

"Oh, come on, Ellie," I replied after minimal reflection. "Savour the moment."

"Of course, Sam. Of course I shall. But don't get caught napping after the re-start."

I was astounded to hear Ellie use a metaphor from soccer, and she read my face with amusement.

"Remember, Sam," she said. "When you've just scored a goal, you're on a high. You're not concentrating. Your nerves haven't settled. Then the opposition takes you unawares and hits back with an equaliser. Just think about it."

Not bad for an elderly, prim widow, I thought.

"Don't worry about him, Ellie," I reassured her, "Penny and I will always be here to support Max. And you of course."

"Thanks, Sam," she smiled. "Yet, you know, in a way Max has been even more restless since you arrived. I think your workplace experience has made him feel as if his ministry's a little too detached and other worldly."

"Oh that's nonsense," I replied vehemently. "Some of us are called to full time ministry, and that usually means way more than full time. Others are called to be part time. One person can't do everything."

"Yes, indeed. You're right. I know you're right. You know you're right. But Max can't see it that way. He feels he should be doing everything. He wants to be all things to all people, like Paul. I know he longs to engage with people outside the church, just as you and Penny seem to be able to."

"Then we'll just have to convince him he's a great priest who's got a back up team with a diversity of gifts," I replied. She looked impressed at my quickness and I didn't let her know that I was just recycling a previously-used phrase. "Ellie", I added, "our company's always subscribed to Belbin's management principle. One person can't do everything, but a team can."

Ellie smiled enigmatically, but I could tell she was as convinced by my analysis as she was unconvinced by Max's mask.

Of course, nothing untoward happened in the following months, yet Ellie's words lingered with me, and I often found myself reflecting on their guileless wisdom.

And, indeed, her counsel was to prove prescient.

3. ALASTAIR:

Another Country

"Traitor. Miserable, pusillanimous traitor," Alastair Crawford muttered *sotto voce*, but not so *sotto* that it couldn't be heard by half of St Finnan's. He was already turning on his heels and striding out of the church hall before the recipient of his anger, Bill Wallace, could react.

It was a discomfiting episode for Penny and me, so soon after we had arrived in Kilfinan and settled into the seemingly benign fellowship of the town's Episcopal church. What made it all the more disquieting, in the view of the Rector, was that Crawford and Wallace had been the best of mates, veritable exemplars of gracious Christian men.

If ever there was an instance of religion and politics being uneasy bedfellows, this was it. The spat had begun in early 2013, when the issue of Scotland's independence had gained momentum and now, a year from the referendum, things were starting to turn unpleasant. It was highly ironic that someone with the name of William Wallace should be the seen as the flagbearer of the Unionist cause, and it was not a role that he courted. But he wanted to make it clear how profoundly he disagreed with the separatists on matters of principle and substance, whilst being no less proud of his Scottish heritage than Crawford or any of his sympathisers.

Crawford, on the other hand, was equally adamant that an historic opportunity had arisen, and one which was unlikely to be repeated during his lifetime. He harboured no fundamental antipathy towards the English – indeed, if he had, he would not have found a spiritual home in the Episcopal church – though he held a deepening disdain for what he saw as their politics of greed and self-interest. There was still sufficient wealth under the North Sea for Scotland to make a decent fist of becoming a separate nation state, though both revenues and time were starting to run out.

I felt curiously distanced from the issue, almost disenfranchised. The Rector of St Finnan's, Max Maxwell, advised me to shrug it off as a temporary political spat, far less serious than those that had divided their flock during the 1980s. However, I spectated the polarisation with disquiet. I would never describe myself as a political animal; my voting intentions are a private matter and I have learned to treat others' in the same way. However, I am aware that, when it comes to political issues, Christians are often passionate to a fault, and I have seen how politics can divide otherwise like-minded brothers and sisters in Christ. The rift between Crawford and Wallace, I sensed, went rather deeper than was desirable. Further, the public animosity which had developed between the two had raked up divisions within the congregation's uneasy truce on the matter.

Penny, for her part, was bemused by the seeming pettiness of it all. For her, gentility started somewhere around York and then continued as far south as Barcelona and Rome, with an eastward extension in the direction of Vienna. At a pinch, she was prepared to tolerate Edinburgh, but otherwise she failed to comprehend why anyone living on this grey Atlantic periphery should want to further isolate themselves from civilisation by decoupling from the rest of the United Kingdom.

Up to the very public spat, the independence issue had been pretty much taboo. You couldn't escape it in the papers or television. There had even been a heated and well attended debate in the local community centre featuring prominent politicians from the opposing factions. But when it came to Sunday morning at St Finnan's, a polite silence was maintained, and the congregation confined their conversations to the appallingly wet winter and health updates on absent friends.

I can't say I was delighted when Max asked – or rather told – me, in his disarming but incontestable way, to preach a sermon on the matter of independence. "Sam," he had said, "you're the ideal person to speak on this. An outsider. You can take a dispassionate view. Offer some words of spiritual wisdom."

I didn't believe him. It was obvious to me that he was ducking the issue because it was too divisive and confrontational. Also, I felt that my interloper status would make me the worst possible person to express a view on the topic. I was on the point of refusing and of upbraiding him for his attempt to lever me into an untenable position. But his manner is so persuasive and affable that he invariably wrong-foots you into agreement. Also, I realised that he had actually been deeply affected by the spat, and was looking for a way to prevent schism. He had long experience, and I credited him with sufficient insight to perceive when his flock needed to hear a particular message. There was no doubt that, behind his benign exterior, he harboured a great depth of passion and intellect.

It was a close call, but I agreed to do the sermon, something which I instantly regretted.

I asked Penny and, to be honest, she wasn't much help. She thought I was stupid for agreeing and that the sermon was inherently unpreachable. "You should steer clear of politics," she asserted. "Especially on politics where you patently don't have any credibility. You were daft to agree. Don't look to me for help."

I harrumphed and strutted off to my study, but didn't argue because she had only confirmed my gut feeling. However, my protestations didn't help the problem to go away; they only compounded it, because now I had incurred the wrath of my wife. And it was wrath born, not of sin, but of rank stupidity, which was more difficult to handle because it only reinforced my image as *Old Makeweight*.

Over tea, I tried to build some bridges by turning our conversation towards theological matters, because I knew she couldn't resist a good discussion. "Do you think I should just say that religion and politics don't mix? Tell people to leave their differences at the door and concentrate on the things we have in common in Christ?"

I didn't really convince myself, but it seemed a decent opening gambit.

She thought for a moment, longer than I'd imagined. But eventually she gave me the answer I'd anticipated, if a little more eloquently than I might have put it.

"What we share in Christ is a commitment to justice, to the poor and disadvantaged. We're inevitably going to be political. And so we're bound to disagree at times."

It isn't the typical response of a marketing consultant, but I've come to expect it.

"Isn't that a rather social view of the gospel?" I replied after a few moments of feigned thought. I knew this was the kind of question to touch on a raw nerve for, whilst she wasn't exactly a hard-line socialist, she disdained my own tepid political allegiances.

She thought hard, almost as if she was being interviewed as an ordination candidate. She had to be careful not to blunder into a minefield of her own making.

"No. It's not about party politics. It's not about a faction. It's about the ultimate goal. We all have different means to the end, and we should respect each others' differences about those means. But we should all seek the same end."

Of course I didn't disagree with her, but decided to toy a little longer. "So, shouldn't Christians take sides in party politics, then?", I added.

Penny answered rather more confidently and quickly than I'd hoped. "Don't, whatever you do in your sermon, lapse into party politics. Don't take sides, just stick to principles. But that doesn't mean individual Christians can't take sides. Just that they should remember to love and respect people on the other side. Provided they're also honest and principled, of course. We may agree about the end, but we're entitled to disagree about the means to the end."

Then she added, as if trying to impress a bishop, "Just provided that we remember the end is to seek the kingdom of God. Justice, righteousness and peace." Of course, she was spot on, even if I thought it sounded uncommonly pious. I conveyed that in my expression, and she smiled in a way that conceded I wasn't such a simpleton after all.

"What about nationalism, though?" I ventured. "That doesn't split people along the usual party lines. It's about identity and self-determination. And about loyalty and unity."

"You're on very thin ice with this one," she said. "Nationalism also has a dark side. You never know what you're going to stir up. Make sure you tread very carefully."

"Perhaps it's better for me to steer clear. Say nothing. Just keep to a safe middle course about justice and freedom. Agreeing about the end, and agreeing to disagree about the means to the end?"

"Yes, you could. It'd be a cop-out. But then that's the church's default position – a cop-out. Why not just go with the herd and give them some pious platitudes?"

"So should I confront the issue and give people some moral guidelines?"

"Risky. It'd sound patronising and judgemental."

"So what do you suggest I do then?", I snapped. I was irritated because she was enjoying the *schadenfreude* of my misguided capitulation to the sermon, and was deliberately letting me stew in my own juice.

"Cop out, then," was her final suggestion.

We both knew this was a non-starter, so I stumped off to the study to try and draft a sermon.

In the end I prepared a talk that I felt was impeccably balanced and incontestable, prayed over it and rehearsed it carefully. But I was still a bundle of nerves when I got up to speak. It still seemed a terribly bad idea. A classic case of the ill-informed outsider telling insiders what they ought to think. I was certain I would alienate one half of the congregation by preaching politics, and the other half by pontificating on issues about which I knew nothing.

Staring at the faces whilst I was preaching, I sensed that my worst fears were being confirmed.

You can tell when a sermon is going badly by the general shuffling and air of disengagement amongst your audience. At times I wish I was a old-fashioned Presbyterian with a full hour at my disposal, taking a traditional evangelical line and anchoring my viewpoints in a sound scriptural exegesis. The congregation would be duty bound to heed my admonitions or face an eternity of torment. But I'm an Anglican; I had the standard ten minute homily before people started checking their mobile phones to make sure that their watches were correct.

Crawford was there. Wallace was there. Along with most of the congregation, they stared at me with intense expressions on their faces. I put on my most soothingly unctuous and assuaging tone when they started to become restive. I did my best to convince my listeners that they should be politically aware, yet tolerant of fellow worshippers who were committed to different political causes. Even being a Fairtrade church was political, I emphasised, and received some nods of agreement in return. We even had a councillor in our midst I observed, turning my eyes towards Mrs Farquhar and, whilst we might not always agree with her party stance, it was our duty to pray for her to discharge her responsibilities wisely.

Then I turned to the independence issue. I felt a frisson of unease shiver across the transept. Perhaps this was because I had already spoken for seven minutes and there was dismay that I was launching into a topic which would need at least half an hour to scratch the surface.

I started by warning about the dangers of nationalism that we should learn from history. The spontaneous shuffling and looks of consternation led me to accelerate my observations on the entirely respectable pedigree of self-determination. This in turn drew worried expressions from half of the congregation who wondered if I was about to justify the case for separation. I skipped through my notes, reducing them to a few disconnected observations about loyalty and multiple identities. After eleven and a half minutes I fast forwarded to the conclusion that, whatever the outcome of the referendum, we needed to carry on living peaceably with each other and that we should refrain from harbouring grudges. Indeed, the church might have an important role in reconciling a divided nation following the referendum.

As I stepped down I sensed that the congregation had received little spiritual nourishment from my words. Yet there was a shared feeling of relief – on the congregation's part that I had finished, and on my part that no-one had walked out. I hardly dared to look at Max as I moved round to take up my place at the side, but from the corner of my eye I saw him nod an approving expression in my direction. Evidently he had thought my inept effort rather good, or at least better than he might have done.

The atmosphere at communion was less celebratory than usual but at least no-one refused to receive the cup, though we shared the peace rather stiffly. But what struck me most, as people filed out at the end of the service, was the utter lack of comment on the sermon's content. I think I might have preferred a punch on the nose to their studious politeness and inconsequential pleasantries.

I confess that I succumbed to the same tendency and avoided discussing the sermon with Max and the sundry individuals who remain after the service to clear away chairs and simulacra, and count the collection. Perhaps I should have been brave enough to broach the matter myself, but didn't, and no-one else saw fit to raise it either. There was plenty of discussion about service planning, heating bills and choice of hymns. Perhaps it had just been ill-judged, I thought, to meddle in politics. Perhaps sermons should just confine themselves to more pietistic matters.

Penny and I rarely discuss my sermons – which she generally feels are a touch superficial – so it was little surprise when we managed to avoid talking about it over lunch. We prattled on about how best to take advantage of the fact that, this being the third Sunday of the month, there was no evening service to rush back for.

We settled for a long walk along the front, ending up at the Harbour Lights café where we watched a flotilla of dinghies racing in the stiff breeze. The sermon was, thankfully, becoming a distant memory and we were now far more interested in discussing our plans for the next week.

But at that point, Alastair Crawford and his partner Sinead walked into the café. A little to my surprise, they nodded congenially and chose the table next to us.

"You must be Sam," said Sinead leaning across to me. I'd heard a little about her, enough to know that she was even more of a political animal than Alastair and had scant interest in spiritual matters. "Alastair tells me you played a blinder this morning."

For a moment, I assumed it was irony, but she sounded perfectly serious and didn't look the type to be deferential out of mere politeness. I wasn't sufficiently self-deprecating to deny the compliment.

"It's kind of you to say so. I feared it was a bit of a lead balloon". Penny maintained an inscrutably Sphinx-like smile.

"Oh no, believe me, I've been hearing about it all afternoon. Someone's dared to mention the unmentionable. Shake the congregation out of its stupor."

In truth, I had never intended any such thing, but was prepared to learn that that was how it had been received.

"Well, I don't think it was especially fiery," I replied. "I was trying to be scrupulously balanced, you know. I'm not going to take sides, not publicly at least. The only side I take is that Christians should engage with the real world."

" Absolutely," chimed in Alastair. "Now don't get too big-headed about it. It wasn't that great a sermon. More like the proverbial dog dancing on its hind legs – what's surprising," he laughed, "is not that it does it well, but that it does it at all."

I should have felt more crestfallen than I actually did.

I settled back to enjoy the view and drift into a more anodyne conversation. But Penny upped the ante.

"So, are you going to kiss and make up with Bill," she asked, her face full of candour and optimism. I think she was genuinely hurt by Alastair's response.

His face summoned the atavistic wrath of his ancestors; his brow suddenly filled with a righteous, zealous anger.

"That Pharisee," he retorted. "He's like a publican and tax-gatherer, collaborating with the Romans, doing their dirty work. We've a historic moment to be free. Free to make our own choices without kow-towing to an imperial power. I'll leave the church rather than sit in the same pew as him."

Penny was simultaneously cross with herself at misjudging the situation and baffled by his take on history. She was a modernised Social Democrat at heart, and heard in him the knee-jerk rhetoric of old-style socialists against the ubiquitous evils of capitalism, only this time directed against Westminster imperialism.

"Oh, come on," she said, flapping desperately to maintain a degree of authority, "it's not that bad."

In return, she received a finger-jabbing diatribe from Sinead about colonial exploitation. "Look at what's happened to Kilfinan over the years. First the landlords come and clear the people off the land so they can have grouse moors for the rich. Then the forestry moves in and all the profits go to southern tax-dodgers. Then the oil rig fabricators come in because we've got deep water, bring in mobile construction teams for a few years, then they clear off. Then Thatcher kills off the shipbuilding industry and all our suppliers go out of business. Then the Americans move out of the naval base. Then our oil and gas are plundered in a generation and the money goes down south. Just look about you. Run down shops, young people leaving, twenty percent unemployment, families living on state benefits. And all for why? Because we can't make our own decisions. And all because of yellowbellies like Bill Wallace."

I didn't feel it was quite like that, but was determined not to start taking sides. After all, it was refreshing to meet someone who was actually passionate about something. And I didn't like to say anything critical because it might put Sinead even more off the church, and Alastair might side with her. I would like to pretend that I was deeply concerned about Alastair's capacity for Christian love, but really I think I was just nervous that we might lose a member and his monthly standing order.

I was aware that people around us were eavesdropping, and at one time this would have been enough to make me clam up. But the experience with Lloyd – combined with my new and more official church role – made me less self-conscious about broaching spiritual matters in public. To my surprise, Alastair didn't seem to mind at all, whilst Sinead clearly enjoyed the sport. Very well then, in for a penny, in for a pound.

"Now I can't entirely agree with you," I continued. I expected angry glowers in return, but confrontation was evidently bread-and-butter to Alastair and Sinead, and they didn't seem in the slightest offended. "Christians should be far more united by what they share in common than divided by their disagreements. However sincere those disagreements might be."

The rest of the café had gone unnaturally quiet. Our contretemps was evidently interesting rather than embarrassing.

"Look," Penny interjected, in a way that I hadn't expected. "Think about want the old hymn says. 'Jesus calls us from the worship of the vain world's golden store, From each idol that would keep us, saying, *Christian, love Me more.*' And Paul tells us to be of the same mind, maintaining the same love, united in spirit."

I wasn't accustomed to her taking such an evangelical line, but instinctively reinforced the point. "Absolutely. Look how Paul told the church at Corinth not to be divided. He was deeply upset by their quarrels. Of course, I'm sure they had big political differences, but he was upset when these were bigger than their common cause. He would have also reminded them that governing authorities have, for one purpose or another, been established by God and should command a degree of respect. Of course, that can lead us to different conclusions."

This clearly made everyone in the café pause for thought, not just Alastair. And then Sinead said something even more surprising, if in a slightly mischievous tone of voice.

"Shouldn't you Christians love your neighbour as yourself?"

Clearly all those school assemblies hadn't been entirely lost on her.

Alastair forced himself to calm down. He'd had a lifelong grounding in the scripture which had left a deep mark. He thought about what we'd said, and the enveloping silence suggested he wasn't alone.

"Okay, Sam," he said in a conciliatory way. "But why are you taking this out on me? Why not on Bill?"

"Because it was you who happened to walk into the café," I quipped in a jocular tone, which fortunately struck the right chord. "Don't worry. If Bill had walked into the café I'd have given him grief.

And I promise that I'll find occasion to give him grief in the near future."

That lightened the mood considerably, and we carried on chatting for another hour about what a wonderful place Kilfinan was despite its historical oppression and how we would all like to join the dinghy sailors out on the sea loch if only we had the skills and the time. The rest of the patrons resumed their previous conversations, and both the independence issue and religion returned to the realms of taboo. Still, I'm sure that, privately, people's minds would continue to pick over what we had said.

I was true to my word and gave Bill a friendly earbashing one evening after he'd finished helping at our youth group. He took it graciously.

Penny and I remained assiduously neutral on the political pros and cons of independence, but deeply concerned that the church had a healing role to play where there was polarisation. We didn't want to stop Christians being passionate about social and economic issues. If they remained coolly rational, they'd probably become humanists. And if we just insisted that Church should be a safe place where we can set our earthly differences aside then we'd become an anodyne holy huddle, dodging the real issues. What if Wilberforce had kept the peace so that his church could be a safe place? Would he have spent forty-odd years of his life campaigning for the abolition of slavery? Church shouldn't too safe, even if we end up saying some uncharitable things about each other. After all, didn't Paul have some uncharitable things to say about Barnabas after he'd wimped out under pressure?

We prayed about the situation regularly, that we might be given an opportunity to help reconciliation. To be honest, it was the first time that we'd seriously prayed together about anything in ages.

A few weeks before the referendum I noticed that Bill and Alastair were chatting at the end of a service. 'Chatting' is probably an insufficient word; there was a palpable edge to their conversation, but at least it wasn't openly argumentative.

I went up to them and, after a few sociable gambits, something inside me told me to produce a coin from my pocket. As soon as I'd done it, I realised why.

"Look chaps, who's head's on the pound?", I asked.

"The Queen's of course," Alastair conceded. Despite being a republican, he reluctantly endorsed the Nationalists' promise to keep a British monarch as Head of State. After all, the Union of Crowns had a longer history than the Union of Parliaments.

"Then render therefore unto Caesar the things which are Caesar's, and unto God the things that are God's. At the end of the day," I said, looking straight into their eyes and with a degree of assurance, "politics has something of the variable whilst the church has something of the constant." I wasn't entirely sure what it meant myself, but it sounded clever and I'd said it with sincerity.

"Aye, you're right," said Alastair. Then he turned to Bill, shook his hand and said, "Good luck."

Bill looked him in the eye. "Good luck," he replied.

4. CLARE:

Using Your Loaf

Penny is a healthy eater, one might almost say faddy. Having despaired at the processed meals which lined the shelves of Kilfinan's supermarkets, she became a progressively more adventurous cook and latterly even badgered me into acquiring a degree of culinary competence myself. I am not given free rein, however. She counts our calories rigorously and restricts, though not without a degree of imagination and creativity, our diet to wholesome combinations of vegetables, fish, poultry and occasional lean beef.

Having witnessed the burgeoning waistlines of some of my colleagues I have readily succumbed to her regime. Only very rarely do I now indulge in a Danish pastry at coffee break.

Pastoral work here has presented me with something of a challenge, as my occasional courtesy calls to parishioners' homes invariably involve being presented with a bewildering choice of biscuits and traybakes. Fortunately, my visits are far less frequent than those required of Max, which goes a long way to explain his perpetual battle against circumference.

Penny's first foray to Mackies, the local bakers, to buy a freshly baked organic wholemeal loaf was unsuccessful. She was dismayed at the panorama of sweet and savoury goods on display. She found it even more alarming to witness the relish with which locals depleted the creamy, sugary pastries, and cholesterol-laden pies, such that by mid-morning the shelves were largely stripped bare.

Jean and Frank – known throughout the town as Ma and Pa Mackie – were longstanding stalwarts of St Finnan's. They were a generously proportioned couple as you might imagine and, whilst their larger-than-life personalities were not to everyone's taste, they generally well liked amongst their fellow citizens and worshippers.

Penny did little to conceal her coolness towards them, but I could not indulge myself in such selectivity. Despite the Mackies' rather extravagant and opinionated manner, I found them to be perfectly decent and hard working paragons, not to mention their generosity in relation to the collection plate.

The Mackies were a Kilfinan institution who seemed likely to go on forever. But then Clare and Nick arrived.

I was delighted when Clare introduced herself to me at the end of a service, and pointed to where Nick was standing on the other side of the transept. Max had tipped me off in advance, having received an email from them, and asked if I could detect where they were from. Whilst Clare's accent might have sounded merely 'English' to the local ear, I immediately detected in her voice a West Country burr.

I plumped for Somerset and was pleased when she told me they'd moved up from Bath, "to escape the rat race". The tentacles of London extend almost the entire length of the M4 these days.

They had clearly brought with them a combination of youth, energy, capital from the sale of their home, a small business savviness, and a fondness for contemporary worship. I had a cheerful chinwag with Clare, then moved on to catch up with other communicants, though I watched Penny stalk and then make a beeline for her. I can tell when she's putting on an act and when she's genuinely enthused by people. This was the latter.

Clare was exactly Penny's cup of tea: entrepreneurial, smart and driven, with a spirituality that was risky and inclusive. Perhaps Clare was Penny's alter ego, if she could have returned to her twenties and married someone other than me! It was clear she liked Nick, too. He was charismatic in an unobtrusive sort of way, less prone to flights of fancy than Clare, but with an astute commercial acumen that compensated for his apparent lack of pzazz.

Clare had confided in Penny that they had bought a run-down cottage with a degenerate but recoverable orchard; both had plenty of potential, as the estate agent had assured them. Their business strategy was to exploit a niche market in quality food. They were sure there was a market in 'real' baking – fresh bread, bagels, wholegrain snacks and the like. And this could be complemented by a subsidiary enterprise producing smoothies based on Central Scotland's soft fruit industry, together with a non-alcoholic cider based on the under-utilised local crop of native apple varieties. Their day jobs had been in financial services, but cooking was their real passion and they had spent the last year honing their baking skills around the exigencies of professional lives. Given their capital base, they were confident they could move into profit by their second year.

I was carried along by Penny's enthusiasm after her first meeting with the couple – and by a sneaking admission that a decent food shop wouldn't go amiss hereabouts. There wasn't a quantity problem on Kilfinan's high street but, through our immigrant eyes, it was short on quality. Within a month of the couple's arrival, one of our two newsagents retired and, not finding a family successor for his business, put the shop on the market.

I mentioned it to Nick after a Sunday evening service, only to discover they had already been to view it. The premises were run down and not an ideal shape for a bakery-cum-shop; it bore all the tell-tales of a unit whose owner had lost interest in its upkeep and had scraped by for the past several years on a minimal profit from an unimaginative selection of newspapers, magazines, sweets and tacky souvenirs. On the positive side, it was in a central position and was amidst what, by Kilfinan's standards, were top-end shops. The asking price was higher than they'd expected but, as they seemed likely to be the sole bidders, Nick felt they could get away with a low offer.

It was no surprise when we saw the *Sold* sign go up, nor when, a few weeks later, we saw Nick and

Clare hard at work inside. I tapped on the window and was enthusiastically invited in. Standing with welcome mugs of tea from a Thermos flask we discussed their plans. Although they might have looked like happy, smiley, easy-going dropouts, their sense of business acumen was electric. My own work could be high powered at times, especially when it involved major project funding, so I could tell a really well thought out business proposition when I saw one.

It was patently obvious to me that they were comfortable with and experienced in serious business decisions. They had clearly driven a very shrewd bargain on the price of the premises and spoke about alternative cash flow models in an impromptu manner which conveyed that this wasn't just a carefully rehearsed paper exercise for the bank manager. Besides, I got the impression that it was mostly their own money behind the investment. "We'll be okay provided we only lose our own money; it's when you start losing other people's money that you get into trouble," Clare had said with a grin.

But eclipsing everything was Clare's enthusiasm for baking, especially where there was the possibility of a nutritionally balanced, wholefood option. She was a mine of information about cakes, pastries and pies, but her true passion was for British and continental breads of every description. She took me to the dingy store room at the back of the shop and animatedly showed me where the ovens and work surfaces were going to go as if she could already visualise them gleaming. Nick spoke equally enthusiastically, if a little more softly, about their sideline in fruit beverages.

Penny was bowled along by Clare's enterprise, and was soon eagerly exchanging tips on how to market the new business. "When you look at the realistic competition in the area," she suggested, "there simply isn't any. There's so much untapped potential, you could be sitting on a gold mine." She continued to give Clare free marketing advice with unprecedented generosity, doubtless in the hope of signing her up as a future client, though I did ever so gently chide her about the dangers of showing favouritism towards individual parishioners.

A couple of weeks later, after the Sunday morning service, I introduced Clare to the Mackies on account of their common interests. I retreated to the church door for the customary hand shaking, and noticed from afar that their conversation was polite but formal. It seemed that there was no real point of connection after all, and perhaps I should not have been surprised. Just because we share the same faith doesn't mean to say that we'll automatically be lifelong friends. Nor because we share the same occupation will be necessarily be on the same economic wavelength. Of course, they were different characters, with different aims in life, orienting their businesses towards different markets.

Clare and Nick's new shop, *Manna*, was launched with a well conceived – and especially well marketed – fanfare one Saturday morning. Carefully gauged articles and adverts in the press were reinforced with an eye-catching flyer distributed extensively throughout the peninsula. Not cheap, but very astutely targeted and executed. Clare was rushed off her feet in the shop with Nick flat out behind the scenes, and Penny and I felt guilty about not lending a helping hand as we queued up for our free focaccia, but somehow they kept upright and smiling for nine hours without a break. We were not surprised when they didn't make it to church the following morning.

The feedback from questionnaires was exceptionally positive and Penny helped Clare to analyse the responses and refine their product mix. Trade was brisk on the following Monday and there were some complaints that certain products had run out too early, whilst they were left with inevitable surpluses of other items, but the imbalance was quickly rectified in the following days. It was clear from custom in the weeks which followed that the business was meeting its early targets; there was a viable market, even in this far-flung outpost.

Not that we should get carried away about a potential revolution in eating habits. Clare politely but firmly declined suggestions from some clients that *Manna* should stock traditional specialities with a high fat and sugar content, something which doubtless cost her friends and profits. Yet Clare did not treat the suggestions flippantly. She was acutely aware of the thin line between personal ideals and market realities; nor did she want to risk negative branding by alienating influential residents. Thus it was that, by the end of the summer season, when Kilfinan's population is swollen by visitors, *Manna* had achieved a healthy turnover and had engaged two part-time employees.

Indeed, one of the part-timers was a member of our youth fellowship, and she was an amusing and indiscreet commentator on the couple's interpersonal qualities. They were clearly driven by Christian values, and were constantly alert to sharing their faith in surprisingly frank ways, but also took a strict line on the need for prudence and hard work, never short of a proof text or two from Proverbs.

One of the key features of change in regard to social custom and practice is that it tends to be exceedingly slow, yet equally sure. Once set in motion, the wheels of progress can be difficult to reverse.

And so it proved in Kilfinan. What might have been an unexceptional tale of two bakeries at opposite ends of the town, keeping themselves to themselves, became a saga of diverging fortunes. Small local inflexions in loyalty and patronage were compounded by government health initiatives and changing attitudes. *Manna* became an ever more attractive shop, buoyed by an enthusiastic clientele of self-catering tourists. It expanded into neighbouring premises which had subsequently become vacant, and hired additional staff. Meanwhile, Mackies, so long a local institution, started to look unexciting and, even worse, unloved. Its gradually diminishing clientele increasingly comprised the elderly and impecunious. It was not long before they had to lay off their only remaining employee, a 'saturday girl' who was also a member of our junior church.

The girl's bitterness was revelatory. She blurted out the story to us one evening at youth group. She told it as if it were her own, though it was clearly a received account. The Mackies were wonderful people who treated her with the milk of human kindness. They had served the town and the Episcopal church generously and unstintingly for several decades. But their business was being ruined by unscrupulous competitors who were deliberately poaching their best customers. And to cap it all, these people were unmarried and living in sin, yet described themselves as Christians. Ma and Pa had worked hard all their lives and were now scarcely able to look forward to retirement, with their business income and the value of their premises falling off rapidly.

To be honest, this took us by surprise. We had known that *Manna* was doing well and had built up a loyal client base, including ourselves. But I had not appreciated how much it had impacted on the Mackies. Surely generations of eating habits had not been so quickly undermined by our parvenu couple? The Mackies had been the mainstay of pie suppers, high teas and school lunches for decades and it had never occurred to us – though admittedly we'd never really thought about it – that this wouldn't remain the case through to the end of their working lives.

Yet it emerged that, although the Mackies' footfall had declined only a little, profits had fallen sharply. When we looked more closely at their shop, we saw that it was patronised by an increasingly residual clientele who wanted somewhere to pass the time of day. By now, we had discovered that, ever since the post office had been downgraded to a shelf in the local supermarket, there was nowhere for people of a certain age and disposition to chew the fat, exchange opinions and garner local information. The coterie of pensioners who once gossiped around the stacks of passport and driving licence application forms, had now relocated themselves to Mackies. There, they would talk for Scotland, occupy floorspace and end up buying a solitary pastry with a profit margin of a few pence. What appeared to be a thriving traditional retail outlet was in fact a zombie business barely covering its costs.

It wasn't long before I was chatting to Pa Mackie at the church door and, on asking him how he was, was met with a diatribe about unchristian rivals destroying his livelihood. Embarrassed by the collateral damage his outburst might have on departing communicants, I managed to keep the peace by inviting him and Ma round for a cuppa that afternoon.

Penny was the epitome of Kilfinan hospitality and had prepared a plate of home-baked patisseries which would have impressed the professionals and certainly amazed me. Ma and Pa tucked in with gusto, but barely had they swallowed their first mouthfuls, when they began to give vent to their grievance. It was abundantly clear that they were in a desperate situation, close to bankruptcy. We had to endure a barrage of criticism about the church's disinterest in their plight. Inwardly, I protested the injustice of being the butt of their criticism – why should they direct their wrath at me, a part-timer with a demanding weekday job? Yet, rationally, I also felt they had a point.

This was a situation that had been developing over a lengthy period, and perhaps it was our duty to have noticed. I really couldn't see how to help them, and there were occasions when I looked despairingly in Penny's direction, only to realise that she too was lost for a response.

Fortunately, Pa Mackie retrieved the immediate situation by apologising for his outburst, admitting it was unfair, and we both replied by saying that of course we didn't mind and it was a good opportunity to get the matter off their chests.

I trust that we parted friends, and the deposits of cream above Pa's upper lip suggested that they had appreciated our hospitality.

But it left us wondering about the challenges of reconciling business ethics with Christian charity, something which stalked our conversation for the remainder of the day. The easy solution, as we reminded ourselves, was for the church just to retreat from the world of competition and wealth-creation, and stick instead to pious works and charity. And we quickly realised that there could be just as many problems when business organisations styled themselves as cooperative rather than competitive.

"Of course, we need to love our neighbour. Perhaps we should spotted sooner that the Mackies were in need of the church's support," I ventured.

Penny thought at length. Eventually she asked, "But who is our neighbour? Is my business competitor my neighbour? And if so, should I back off if I'm damaging their business? Or should I set out to capture a share of the market, even when it's at someone else's expense? You need to be ethical, but you can't just be soft."

She was thinking aloud and didn't really expect an answer, which was fortunate because I hadn't got one.

I knew there were times in my own work, for a big company, when business ethics were difficult enough. Times when you had to be creative with the truth when bidding for a contract, times when you poached funds from other divisions, times when you had to turn a blind eye to health and safety lapses, to mention but a few. I try to act as morally as reasonably possible, and gather I have a reputation amongst junior staff for being approachable and supportive. But almost every day there seems to be something which gives me twinges of conscience. I could only imagine what it must be like for owners of small businesses out there in a ruthless market with wafer-thin profit margins, where every day you are having to steal the wind from your competitor's sails just to survive.

I know that Penny has a peculiar attachment to a particular passage in Luke 16 which appears to commend the worldly wise – where a master rewards his dishonest manager for acting shrewdly. Jesus seems quite frustrated that 'the people of this world' are more shrewd than 'the people of the light'. Of all the difficult passages in the New Testament, this is one that has caused us the most problems in understanding how to engage with the competitive world of commerce. It would just be too easy to cocoon our faith in a naïve and innocent little enclave.

But is Jesus suggesting that God wants us to be entrepreneurs? Should spiritual entrepreneurs be driven by the same thirst that drives successful businesspeople? Is it right for a Christian to threaten a competitor's business even if their competitor is less good? And if we dodge the issue of mammon would businesspeople just see us as pious and impractical? This is a dilemma we've never been able to fathom, but which we're going to keep exploring because we're experiencing it at first hand.

As chance would have it, Max mentioned that Clare and Nick had asked him to pay them a visit, and I suggested that I could go in his stead. I didn't want to confront them, not least because they'd been a breath of fresh air at St Finnan's, and Penny and Clare were great friends. On the other hand, I didn't simply want to let the matter drop because the Mackies were clearly distressed and I wanted to clutch at anything which might help me to build bridges. I hoped that a chat with the proprietors of *Manna* might at least begin to clarify matters.

When I arrived at their home I was struck by two things. The first was the frugal nature of their accommodation. Often when I go into an older cottage, I discover that it has been stylishly and fashionably converted. But Clare and Nick's sitting room suggested a couple on a straitened budget who had ploughed back everything into their business. Notwithstanding this, the warmth of the welcome more than compensated for the sparsity of furniture. The second was that Clare, dressed rather more casually that I had seen her at church, seemed to be displaying the beginnings of a bump.

"We'll cut to the chase," Clare said, after she had plied me with a cup of Earl Grey and a plate of cranberry and yoghurt cookies. "In view of this," whereupon she patted what was indeed a bump, "we thought it was about time to tie the knot."

"Conceiving first is the wrong way round, perhaps…," started Nick.

"But it's the modern way," I smiled. "Congratulations."

I must admit, it had never really worried me that they weren't married, though doubtless it was one of the reasons why the Mackies together with about a third of the congregation had been cool towards them from the outset.

I explained that, of course, it really was Max with whom they should be speaking, but that I had a pretty good knowledge of the protocols and diary commitments; and of course Penny was now making a significant contribution to the marriage preparation course which would be running again shortly and which we'd like them to take.

Without undue haste, and making sure that all the appropriate pastoral details had been covered, I gently steered the conversation round to business matters.

Sales, not surprisingly, were encouraging, but there were still the inevitable privations and worries of the early phases, when income is barely matching outgoings and you wonder if you've bitten off more than you can chew. Every spare minute had been put into, and every spare pound re-invested in, *Manna*. Thanks to their single minded dedication and sacrifice the business was starting to return a profit despite the commitment of employing staff, and they were now in a position to take things a little easier. There was scope to spend some money on the house, take a holiday – and start a family.

In a roundabout sort of way, I asked them if they saw any conflict between running a profitable business and following the teachings of Jesus. Of course, I made it clear that the question arose from mere curiosity, as something which had always interested me as a businessman. Neither had a moment's hesitation. It was clear they saw *Manna* as a God-given calling which, due to their prudence, had been granted success. They saw their personal sacrifices and risks, and the leap of faith that these had involved, being justly rewarded.

I mused whether, perhaps, this was a convenient case of a prosperity gospel, but they insisted not. They were adamant that their ultimate goal was to be welcomed into eternal dwellings, not to gain friends in this life. In the fullness of time, they might open another bakery or two, but really they were just grateful that God had opened a door which enabled them to work at something they enjoyed in a part of the world they loved. I was sorry that Penny wasn't here to hear them talk about Kilfinan in this way, and I disingenuously suggested that Clare might sing its praises to her some time.

I was struck by their patent sincerity. So I felt confident in asking them whether they'd heard that the Mackies weren't doing so well. For the first time, they exchanged nervous glances.

After a few moments, in which fortunately I didn't need to break the silence by saying something gauche, Nick ventured:

"We've tried not to mention the Mackies. We never intended to compete with them. We tried to offer a different product that would appeal to a different market segment. But they've never stopped bad-mouthing us since we arrived."

Clare picked up the thread, as if forcing herself to sound civil and reasonable.

"We had the impression that they were looking for someone to blame. But they'd just stopped trying. They were getting on. They were waiting for retirement. The business had been inefficiently run for ages. They'd never done any market research. To be honest, we never liked the way they relied on schoolkids going in there at lunchtime to get stodgy pies. Really, from our perspective, it was a business waiting to fail. But we never tried to put them under. We just wanted to appeal to a new market. And then people started coming to us. There's a terribly fine line between a viable business and a failing business, and the Mackies just tipped the wrong side of it. We are tipping just the right side of it, but there's no margin for error."

"Or for sentiment," added Nick, glancing cautiously across to Clare for reassurance. "We can't underplay our own business just because we feel sorry for them," he added.

I tried to judge whether they were being sincere, or merely self-justifying. There's a well-known saying in business that it isn't enough just to show that you're winning, you've got to show that your competitor is losing. It's easy to deliberately undermine the opposition, whilst kidding yourself that you're just being efficient and prudent. On this occasion, probe as I might, I really couldn't tell. I simply bade my farewells, wished them lots of good fortune and God's blessing, and assured them that Max would be speaking to them soon about the wedding.

Penny couldn't help me either. She was so close to the issue, in terms of starting up her own business and being good friends with Clare, that she lacked the capacity to be impartial. Try as she might – and she genuinely gave it lots of thought and prayer – she couldn't elucidate.

As it turned out, matters sort of resolved themselves. The Mackies were close to being able to draw their state pension; they were able to sell their premises and associated accommodation for a reasonable sum, even though they couldn't sell their business as a going concern. Fortunately, they didn't entirely stop attending church, so I was able to shake hands with them one last time and wish them all the best for the future just prior to their departure. They were, inevitably, polite if unforthcoming about their plans and Max told me that they had no wish to continue receiving our church magazine, which is a rather sad postscript to their lifelong contribution to St Finnan's.

Somewhat more happily, Ellie has managed to keep in touch with them and she regularly drops into their new home – I understand a rather pleasant semi-bungalow in Scotland's *costa geriatrica* a little further south-west. She tells me that their plight was not as bad as we'd been led to believe and they had allowed things to get somewhat out of proportion. They have, she thinks, a tidy little nest egg and appear to be comfortably off. Thanks to her persistent but gentle persuasion, they have settled in a small Episcopal church which is local to them; I know it vaguely, and suspect that they will be happy in its close if rather elderly congregation.

Equally happily, Clare is now the proud mother of lively twins – a boy and a girl, so they have an instant family. *Manna* continues to thrive and Clare already has her eye on vacant premises in two neighbouring towns. I just hope she isn't trying to do too much, too soon. Zeal is a wonderful thing in moderation.

Yet, even though things are tidier than they might have been, I am still left to ponder the difficulty of maintaining a balance between the pursuit of God and the pursuit of mammon. Profit margins are small in a town like Kilfinan and the margin between success and failure is fine, so I appreciate that no-one can afford to be too charitable. But what if the Mackies had been in their mid-forties and been forced into bankruptcy? The fallout wouldn't so easily have been contained.

And it also worries me a little that we may have shown a degree of favouritism towards the proprietors of *Manna*. I try hard to avoid making cliques, as such things don't go unnoticed hereabouts.

Should we have taken more of an active interest in the Mackies, and should we have become aware of their predicament earlier? Perhaps we could have shared tips on how to give their business a makeover? Whatever, I don't like to see people who have given a lifetime to the church leave with ill grace.

I was mightily relieved when Ellie assured me that their faith didn't seem to have suffered any permanent damage. And, most revealingly, she went on to tell me how she had detected Ma and Pa's concerns at an early stage, and so had made a special effort to stay in touch with them during their final year in Kilfinan. She had continued to shop at their bakery in its twilight phase, ensuring that her visits doubled as an opportunity "to chat with the Mackies and make them feel that the church valued them". What an unsung saint we have in Ellie!

And as she spoke, my frisson of guilt at not having even noticed her efforts was accompanied by a vague realisation that she had put her finger on a very important point. I haven't quite rationalised it yet, but it's something to do with the idea of value. Prices and profits are obviously essential if we're to stay in business, but even more important is that we centre ourselves and our businesses on the right values.

I'm continuing to struggle with this, just as I'm gaining an admiration for Ellie's perceptiveness and patience. One of these days, in one of her unassuming but revelatory asides, I am sure she will unwittingly explain to me exactly how Christ-centred values can help us to reconcile competition and compassion.

5. MARGARET:

Growing Old Disgracefully

If you wish your daughter to live to a ripe old age, I suggest calling her Margaret. That was certainly an early impression I gained from the penumbra of people who had some degree of connection with St Finnan's. The preponderance of elderly ladies whose name was some variant of Margaret suggested to me that the Lord must have called their otherwise-named contemporaries to be with Him on a selectively premature basis. Either that, or their nominal association with a favourite queen of Scotland had somehow conferred longevity. There were Margaret H and Margaret P, Maggie D and Maggie M, Margie, Mags, Meg, Peggy, Mamie, Greta and even Daisy. Many of these variants had been acquired at school as a counterpoint to the inevitable confusions.

Margaret P must have been eighty if she was a day when I first met her. Church had been her second home since the loss of her husband, especially as her children had departed for Australia and South Africa many years previously. I only recall her missing one meeting of the Women's Group, due to a particularly virulent strain of influenza, and even that was sufficient to set tongues wagging. Though she would never be so rude as to physically displace an interloper at a church service, all the regulars understood that she customarily occupied the aisle seat of the third row on the left, and was not to be usurped. Her name peppered the flower and coffee rotas and, despite her encroaching ailments and infirmities, she insisted on pulling her weight in the magazine distribution and cleaning duties.

After a few months at St Finnan's, Penny and I started to notice a decline in her faculties. Mrs Wolsey, who was only slightly her junior, commented to me at the end of a service that Mrs P had been uncharacteristically sharp with her over the most trivial matter. It hadn't surprised me, because I had noticed in her a recent tendency to become flustered and frustrated.

To cut a long story short, in the space of the next few weeks, Mrs P's physical mobility and character had deteriorated so noticeably that I became deeply anxious one Sunday when she failed to attend morning service. There was an ominous silence when I rang her doorbell afterwards and I feared the worst. But presently I heard a shuffling and muttering, and the door was opened. She beckoned me to come in and thanked me for my visit.

I sat with her in the lounge and offered to make a pot of tea, which she politely declined, aware that it was really time when I should have been heading back to my lunch. There appeared nothing too bad with her mind and body, but it seemed that her spirit had gone, as if getting herself ready in the morning had become too much of an effort.

Miss Tomlinson, her pastoral visitor, kept an especially close eye on her after this, and I wasn't surprised when a couple of weeks later she hinted that it was time for Margaret to consider moving to the Church of Scotland's eventide home at West Haven, our neighbouring township. Letters to her son and daughter resulted in a rebuff from the former and a resentful visit from the latter, dragged away from her own family in Durban.

Her daughter, Patricia, must have been in her fifties but looked much younger. She radiated impatient energy and spoke with a twang which was now more South African than Scottish. She briskly welcomed me in when I called and rather stiffly offered me a cup of tea, which anticipated and received a polite refusal. Within a matter of minutes, during which her mother was pressed into the car with undignified haste we embarked on a tour of local rest homes which she had arranged in an ambitious timetable, despite my advice that there were really only a couple worth considering. She dragged her bewildered mother around half a dozen which were the subject of grumbling about being too dingy, too smelly, too expensive, too impersonal, too badly managed or too neglectful.

Eventually, after a second visit, she settled on the eventide home, which I had strongly recommended to her in the first instance, despite her complaints that it was overpriced and fuddy-duddy. Still, there was little else to be done, in her view, as she informed her mother in a matter-of-fact way. Bags would be packed and the house would be put on the market to defray the costs; there were lawyers to see, arrangements to be made, and a plane to be caught. Patricia instructed me that it was the church's duty to ensure that her mother was regularly visited and to deal with any inadequacies in care standards which might arise.

Within the week, her mother had been bundled to West Haven Eventide Care Home with an essential minimum of clothes and possessions, the remainder having been distributed among local charity shops, and Patricia had seen herself off to the airport without so much as bidding me farewell.

Visiting Margaret the following week, I did wonder if the move had been a little premature. I have seen folk in a far worse condition continue to sleep in their own bed, but what was done was done, and Margaret was far too much of a gentlewoman either to complain about her new place of residence or to make any criticism of her children. However, there was no escaping the fact that that this was a well-mannered (if somewhat deteriorating) woman who had been rudely forced from her home of fifty years into a place where most of the residents were well below her current mental and physical acuity.

Word spread round quickly about her, and I was reasonably confident that her long-standing friends would ensure a steady stream of visitors. I had to assume that this would be the case as I cannot be everywhere at once and certainly could not add visits to West Haven to my list of evening commitments.

As you get older, things seem to pass more quickly. As a teenager, a year seemed an eternity. As a young family man, each year brought a wealth of new experiences. Now, as empty nesters, we barely have time to catch breath between the months, and often cannot even account for where the time has gone. We try to kid ourselves that 50 is the new 30, but we know it is only desperation at the accelerating approach of grey hairs and organic degeneration.

This is by way of a feeble excuse for waking up one morning a year later and for no apparent reason reflecting on the fact that I hadn't so much as visited Margaret once. Was it really so long since I had written to Patricia about how well her mother was settling in and failed to receive a reply? I mentioned Margaret to Penny in the hope that she'd had news through the grapevine, but it was clear she had difficulty even recalling who I was talking about. I spoke to the president of the Women's Group who assured me that Margaret had been visited from time to time, but that she would be delighted to see me if I ever felt like calling in. It was a free evening and I knew Penny would be pleased if I left her to her own devices, so I decided to visit West Haven.

When I was ushered into Margaret's room, what a deterioration met my eyes!

This once loquacious, vivacious, quick-witted, even mischievous woman had become a crouched, vinegary shadow of her former self. She cared little about appearance or personal hygiene. Despite my best efforts, I could elicit little from her, certainly little that wasn't negative or depressing. If *Old Make-*

weight had a forte it was the ability to chatter away about nothing, to make light hearted and inconsequential conversation at the drop of a hat. Try as I might with Margaret, I could get nothing beyond terse and monosyllabic conversation stoppers. She wasn't trying to be rude or to get rid of me; it just mattered nothing to her whether I spoke or not, or whether I stayed or not.

After half an hour of unproductive effort I bade her adieu and elicited a minimal acknowledgement of my departure. I resolved to mention this visit to her former friends in the faint hope that they might be able to re-kindle some sort of spark.

As I was leaving West Haven, the manager buttonholed me at the door and thrust a brochure into my hand, extolling the virtues of the home, and gently browbeating me about a vacancy that needed to be filled on their Board of Trustees. It would, she assured me, be right up my street; my reputation went before me, apparently, as a man of moral virtue and business acumen. She certainly knew how to sweet-talk and, despite my resolve to take on no more commitments, I was persuaded that this post would be as undemanding as it was worthwhile. Even more astonishingly, when I mentioned it to my boss he informed me it was a perfect fit with the company's new Corporate Social Responsibility policy and that I could attend meetings within working hours.

Thus it was, when I attended my first Board meeting, I was able to announce that our company would sponsor two work experience pupils at the care home during the summer vacation. Rarely had I made such a good first impression.

Perhaps I am becoming more irritable as time advances, but I must admit that the pupils sent by Kilfinan Academy to West Haven were not the ones I would personally have chosen. Robert, a terribly likeable but awfully studious and introverted lad, was assigned to the kitchen and office, whilst Elinor was detailed to participate in activities for the residents. Elinor must have had very liberal parents judging by her piercings, and I am at a loss to explain how her hairstyle scraped through school regulations. I greeted her with a bland question about career aspirations and she replied with a slightly nervous smile which suggested that her external appearance was more about herd conformity than serious rebellion.

When I returned for my next, unexpectedly purposeful and productive, Board meeting I spotted Elinor again, chatting to the residents. She was remarkably relaxed and at ease, and her efforts at socialising were met with a surprising degree of humour and tolerance. She had a kind heart, I realised, although from what I heard I doubted whether she had an equally sharp intellect. Anyway, by the end of the afternoon I was considerably reassured about the merits of student placements. With the advance of autumn, Elinor returned to her studies and to her very modest career ambitions.

My periodic attendances as a Board member doubled up as opportunities for pastoral visits to the handful of residents who had a connection with St Finnan's. I can't say that the prospect had filled me with joy. In fact, my visits reinforced an ominous foreboding of what might lie ahead of me in my declining years. Yet this feeling of despond was counterbalanced by the upturn which I saw in Margaret's demeanour.

As usual, I had kept our conversation to routine matters of her current state of health, the quality of her care, and local news. I steered assiduously away from anything that might remotely be considered 'religious', partly because the more secular Board members and management staff would have deemed it unbecoming, and partly because the weekly service was conducted by the local Church of Scotland minister and I was careful not to tread on her toes.

It was left to Margaret to raise religion, from an unexpected direction.

"Do you remember young Elinor?", she asked, as we were enumerating the quirks and idiosyncrasies of her care staff.

"Yes, of course. The Goth."

"Actually, I think she was an Emo," Margaret replied winsomely. My face must have betrayed an expression of incredulity.

"Nice girl. A little scatterbrained but kind at heart. Well, one day she caught me reading your excellent bible study notes on Amos and she asked me what I was reading and I told her about St Finnan's and the house group I used to go to. She seemed stunned, then she said in the sort of facetious upspeak teenagers can display, 'You don't actually believe that stuff do you?' I smiled meekly and was about to tuck the notes away in my handbag when I thought, 'what on

Earth, why don't I give her something to think about for a change?' So I gave her a very robust answer about how ancient people were much wiser than we realised and how it would do politicians good to read Amos because they might learn something important about peace and justice in the world."

"And how did she react to that?"

"Well I just carried on staring her calmly in the eye and her smirk slowly faded. I think she was utterly fazed so after half a minute she just said, 'will that be all Mrs P?' and I said 'yes thank you'. I could see Mr Braithwaite and Mrs Johnson, who were sitting either side, looking at me with the most curious expressions, and then there was Mrs Lamont" – she nodded discreetly across the room where a very elderly lady was quietly snoozing – "who's very religious and looked like she was going to say something important, but couldn't quite find the words. And I could hear Elinor giggling away in the corridor with Robert afterwards, but what did I care. I'm entitled to be awkward and embarrassing at my age."

It was an unusual conversation gambit but I was most encouraged, because Margaret had suddenly become animated, and seemed positively lively and interested. I tried to think of a way in which to sustain our conversation, but Margaret beat me to it.

"You see, Elinor and I had quite a few conversations about the church after that. None of them very long – I think she was a little embarrassed. But the day before she went back to school, she brought me in this delightful little wooden cross. She'd made it herself – she was very keen on craftwork you know.

And later on, Mrs Johnson, who has to be one of the grumpiest people on the planet, actually smiled and congratulated me about giving the younger generation a lesson in values."

I chuckled openly at the idea of Mrs Johnson cracking a smile, though quietly I was imagining Elinor carefully crafting her cross.

"D'you know", Margaret continued, "I think it was the first time in my life that I'd witnessed. It's something I'd always been terrified of, but when I did it, it came easily and naturally. Imagine waiting over 80 years to do something for the first time and then you discover it was nothing to be afraid of after all."

Not only was Margaret happier than I'd seen her for ages, but she was also more coherent and rational.

"Would you like me to take you bungee jumping?" I asked.

"No, nothing like that!" She laughed until I was afraid she'd choke. "I've no great desire to leave the confines of West Haven at the moment. But since then, I've found opportunities to speak to two of the care staff and I don't know how many visitors about my faith. It's surprising how the opportunities arise. A little mention about the weekly service here and a comment on the new Baptist minister there. Have you met him, by the way? I think he'll be a wonderful asset to Kilfinan. And when you don't ram things down people's throats, it's surprising how receptive they are. People say I'm looking different these days. Do you think I am Sam?"

I said that I thought she seemed a new person, and long may it continue.

Actually, it did continue, much to my surprise. Her change of energy, contentment and outlook proved not to be the nine day wonder I had feared. Margaret may be a little frailer and more forgetful these days, but I lose track of her anecdotes about sharing the gospel. It hadn't occurred to me that there was such a ministry to be had in a place like this, and yet people here need spiritual support as much as anybody. Perhaps even more so given their increasing proximity to the next world.

I must give credit to the management at the care home. I was quite annoyed when they first asked me to join the Board. I have to be very selective in the tasks I take on, otherwise they would just grow like Topsy, and I was particularly sceptical about adding West Haven to my list of commitments. But, actually, I think the management had given careful consideration to someone, other than a minister of religion, who might add to the spiritual dimension to their work.

And what a revelation it has been for me. I had seen rest homes as twilight places in which the church's role was to help people fade away gracefully. I hadn't seen them as hubs of outreach.

Margaret P has taught me that God is an equal opportunities employer when it comes to age. Our antiquity is clearly no barrier to either communicating or receiving the good news. Look at Sarah and Elisabeth. And look at the numerous reference to the link between age and wisdom in Proverbs. Of course, wisdom doesn't always go with age nor folly with youth. But Mrs P has taught me a lot about wisdom lately. There is a particular type of knowledge in her eyes that hasn't been gathered from books or sermons, and she has a well of refreshment that compensates for the absence of her family.

St Finnan's is fortunate in having a relatively balanced age pyramid. But of course, as with most churches, we have a skew towards the elderly, and in the foreseeable future Penny and I will join their ranks. I should preach something for their ears in particular. But of course I also need to say something that will connect with the younger people. Mrs P has just given me an idea for an especially worthwhile sermon.

6. JAMES:

Building The House

One of the first things that strikes visitors to Kilfinan is the absence of cookie cutter housing estates. With the exception of Kilfinan House itself – a medieval domestic castle standing in its own grounds a short distance from the town centre – there is nothing genuinely old.

The centre itself consists mostly of Victorian red sandstone tenements with ground-level shops, generally still in a reasonable state of repair. Towards the seafront, a mixture of Victorian and Edwardian villas, most of which have now been subdivided into self-contained units, compete for the most scenic views seawards. Higher up the slope to the landward side of the main road are more villas, often ornamented with bay windows and mock baronial turrets, from which Victorian shipmasters would have watched their vessels sailing to and from Glasgow.

As the town thins out in either direction along the strip of flat land beside the coast, a greater diversity of more modest but individually designed sandstone villas occupy generous plots in gardens that range from the manicured to the tumbledown. Here and there, modern kit-built, harled bungalows and houses have filled the gaps between or behind the older houses, whilst occasional pockets of speculative development and social housing have been discreetly tucked away.

On an elevated plot, enjoying a prime view over the harbour, one cannot fail to notice a very recent addition to the townscape. Its uncompromisingly modern angular lines, constructed from sustainably sourced timbers and reinforced glass, have been designed in a way that allows it to sit sympathetically against the hillside, yet without making any concessions to the local vernacular. It is clearly the house of someone who has achieved their dream.

For some people dreams remain a fantasy, but for others there is a turning point when design starts turning into reality. When I first met James Cleland, he had reached such a point.

I had just finished officiating at my second service during Max's unofficial mini-sabbatical and was mingling with the congregation, trying desperately to put into practice what I'd learned about techniques for remembering names and their accompanying faces. James was engaged in avid discussion with two other men of a similar age, poring over some document or other. Although their body language made it clear they did not want to be interrupted I felt it necessary to introduce myself. Males under the age of forty are something of an endangered species at St Finnan's and I was keen to show my interest in them.

James at first conveyed irritation as I intruded on their huddle, and he wore the expression of someone for whom the service had been a necessary evil. It transpired they were looking at site plans for a new house, though I felt it was a moot point whether he was soliciting their advice or merely showing off. Looking at the extravagant designs I was extremely surprised to hear it had recently been granted planning consent, a sentiment which would have been tactless to express. James edged to shoulder me out, but when I asked some rather technical questions about site excavations and bearing capacity his pained expression became more tolerant. On adding that my background was in construction, he quickly levered me into the cabal.

The proposed house was at the leading edge in terms of technology. Passive solar gain and natural ventilation were optimised for the climate, ambient music and Wi-Fi were distributed throughout, there were ensuite wetrooms and a lavish kitchen organised round a central island. The roof was replete with solar panels, whose grey lustre complemented the charcoal stain of the timber cladding and tinted glass fascias.

I raised some questions about the costs and James spotted that I was politely avoiding direct questions about how he was affording it.

"Monica and I aren't millionaires," he ventured jokingly, and from the reactions on his friends' faces I could see this was an understatement. "But we've had this dream that, as soon as the kids were old enough to keep themselves amused, we'd build our perfect house. Right here overlooking the shores of Loch Finnan."

"And you're able to do all this with the local building contractors?" I asked, trying to limit my disbelief to a mild degree of scepticism.

"Oh, no", he replied. "We're doing most of the building work ourselves. It's the only way we can make it affordable. We'll get some help with wiring and plumbing, maybe plastering, but this is going to be a self-build project."

I noticed that he dressed well – way better than one could kit oneself out from Kilfinan shops – and that he spoke in a slightly affected but mercifully comprehensible West-End-of-Glasgow accent. He didn't strike me as a typical builder.

"How long do you reckon on it taking you?"

"A year, maybe a bit less if the weather's good, but probably a little more."

I raised my eyebrows at his optimism. If this had been his umpteenth self-build, I might have agreed. I detected from his friend's expressions that they shared my apprehension, perhaps even that they were humouring him. But I also got the impression that James was a tough cookie and not someone to stand being gainsaid.

"We're selling our cottage to raise the capital and we'll live in a caravan on the plot. No point in wasting precious funds on the absolute best, but there are some perfectly decent second hand ones for sale."

"Yes, I've known people who did the same," I continued, stopping short of summarising their plights.

"How do Monica and the children feel about it? You don't mind if I call your wife Monica, do you?"

"Not at all. It's a pity she isn't here to meet you, but she didn't feel like coming today. Not feeling terribly spiritual and preferred the idea of a duvet day, like the kids. I mean, they aren't wildly keen on the prospect, but Monica knows it's the only way she's ever going to get a house like this. She knows there'll be privations and it'll mean working every evening and weekend for a year, but she's up for it. And the kids know it'll be worth a fortune and that one day it'll be theirs."

"Well, it's been good to meet you," I said. "Hope it doesn't mean you'll be too busy to keep coming to church."

James gave me a wry smile and a nod by way of reply. His friends reciprocated. Then I headed off to shake hands with the remains of the departing flock.

I didn't see James for a few weeks after that, though his absence gave me an opportunity to get to know his friends better, and to discuss the possibility of a men's prayer breakfast on Saturdays.

When James did re-appear, it was in an upmarket new saloon, gleaming freshly in the wintry low-angle sunlight. Monica and a precocious-looking girl exited the passenger side whilst James found a parking space. I gauged Monica to be late-thirties, close in age to James, and clearly conscious about her appearance. The girl looked too cool for church; but then I remembered our Junior Church leader had organised a visit from a noted Christian blues singer, and this had evidently sparked off considerable interest among the older children whose attendance had faltered. I watched Monica selectively greet a few professional couples in the congregation and then choose a corner of relative solitude. Whilst waiting for James, she occupied herself with skimming the weekly notice sheet whilst the girl resolutely stared at her smartphone.

At the end of the service, I tried not to pounce on them with indecent haste. But I was keen to button-hole them because they were one of the few families that I hadn't, by then, got to know tolerably well.

"Hello James", I said, intercepting him as he strolled towards the door. "And you must be Monica. Great to see you."

"Delighted. I've heard a lot about you," said Monica. She sounded a little rehearsed, but perfectly civil. "We're waiting for Alicia to come out from junior church."

"Is she an only child?"

"No, there's Rory, but we couldn't talk him into coming today. He's got prelims coming up. He would have actually come but was worried about revision."

James's expression, I felt, conveyed a view that this was a generous interpretation of Rory's absence.

"I remember it well," I chuckled, more sincerely than they could have imagined because it was indeed less than a year since I'd been taking my readership finals.

"How are the preparations for the house coming along?" I enquired.

"Nearly there" James interjected. "Completion on the sale of our cottage should be going through next week and the caravan's on site."

"And how are you looking forward to your temporary home?"

Monica wrinkled her nose disagreeably. "Not terribly" she readily admitted. "But James keeps reminding me it's the only way I'll get the house I want. He's right, of course."

I spotted the pre-teen that must be Alicia emerging from the hall, alongside a vaguely familiar daughter of another sporadically attending family.

"Hi Siobhan," said James to the other girl, "joining us for lunch?" She smiled and cosied up to him self-assuredly.

"We'd better be off" said Monica, adding politely, "See you soon".

But we didn't. I wasn't surprised. I knew exactly how much effort was involved in a self-build, especially for the novice. I also knew the amount of psychological and emotional effort involved. For a couple to succeed at it they really had to be committed; not just to the project, but to each other. And for a Christian couple to succeed at it and remain actively engaged in a church fellowship would be especially challenging.

As winter turned into early spring, I watched their site start to take shape. I saw the excavators move in to level out the foundations. I also saw the variable West Coast weather take its inevitable toll, and the bricks and timber lying in piles for several weeks. I saw walls make painfully slow progress, and even some incipient walls being demolished and re-started.

I hadn't seen any of the family at church for many months. But I had heard anecdotally that the children had been in some minor trouble with the police. I didn't probe further: it was hearsay and it was none of my business anyway, but I couldn't entirely filter out wagging tongues.

The skeleton of the house evolved in fits and starts. I noticed deliveries arrive and traders' vans come and go. Occasionally I spotted James with some other men, whose faces I couldn't make out from a distance, hard at work. They carried on far into the long summer evenings with which we are blessed at this latitude.

Even so, the house was nowhere near finished by autumn when some truly appalling weather set in. Piles of building materials remained beneath tarpaulins whilst rainwater streamed in rills down the saturated hillside. Another thing I noticed was that the classy saloon I'd spotted outside the church that winter morning now stood by itself in the driveway. A second car which had previously been there was now conspicuous by its absence.

By November, it was clear that whoever was living in the caravan had hunkered down for the winter.

I wondered whether I should visit, but I had no mandate to. Officially, the address didn't exist so far as the church was concerned. The family wasn't on our magazine distribution list, which would normally have been my pretext for an impromptu visit, nor had James and Monica ever officially become members.

I spoke to some of James's friends, but they were noncommittal, even evasive, though they had apparently been involved in the building parties at times. When I innocently asked how the house was progressing, it was clear that they hadn't actually been on the site for several weeks. They were sure that if James wanted a visit, he would let me or Max know.

Equally, even the best connected members of the women's group could supply me with few hard facts about Monica. And the youth group leaders knew little about Alicia or Rory beyond general hearsay.

I convinced myself that the family was like many others on the fringe of the church, wanting to maintain a connection without ever really being involved. When we were in Lincolnshire – where a desire to send children to the local Church of England school resulted in a wide penumbra of nominal adherents – the situation had been even more commonplace.

Next spring, the house began to take shape more fully and by the autumn the exterior was impressively complete. Even so, the spasmodic arrival of tradesmen's vans indicated that there was much finishing-off to be done internally, and the caravan clearly remained occupied throughout a second winter. Actually, I'd have loved to have volunteered my services to James. I'm stuck in meetings most of the time nowadays and long to muck in on an actual building site. But there are only so many hours in the week and any prolonged absence from domestic commitments wouldn't have been appreciated by Penny.

March passed like a flash and Lent was almost over when one evening, as I was deep in concentration on material for our house group, I was roused by a ring at the door.

I was surprised to see James. He looked, perhaps, a little older. Craggy and lean, certainly fit and well exercised, wearing loose fitting jeans and a rather too youthful tee-shirt. Bearing in mind the length of time since our previous meeting, I think he was a little surprised that I recognised him instantly.

"James!" I beamed. "How good to see you. Do come in."

He looked pleased and, from his controlled and firm expression, I couldn't have anticipated what was to follow. Penny was in the next room; I was aware she'd sized up the situation but left us to our *tête-à-tête*, not least because she was busy preparing a report for a client.

James seemed sociable and chatty; fortunately, a fresh coffee had just been filtering and he welcomed a mug. We went through to the conservatory and took a seat.

"Is this just a social visit or is there something special you want to talk about?" I asked after initial pleasantries had been exchanged.

He brushed off the suggestion that there was anything amiss. Of course, it was no more than a casual visit to keep in touch with St Finnan's and to apologise that he hadn't been seen for such a time. But within a minute, the words were sticking in his throat and the laddish confidence of his expression started to fade.

Trying hard to control a tremor in his voice, he told me how the children had distanced themselves, glad to be freed from the rein of parental attention. And then how Monica had refused to stay in the caravan for a second winter and how she'd never wanted a flash house anyway, which of course he vehemently disputed. And how one evening she had stormed out with the children, but the children in turn had stormed out to stay with some nearby cousins. According to James's account, Monica had become self-obsessed with her social circles and work. So he had buried himself in his project, dedicating his life to the pursuit of the perfectly designed and located modern house.

To cap it all, a television company had agreed to feature their house in a programme about self-builds. He'd forgotten all about it because the deal had been struck when they first moved into the caravan. He's assumed they had lost interest, but a researcher had turned up a couple of weeks ago to run through the schedule. Worse still, they had wanted to capture them as the perfect family; but now they were even more excited by a human interest story about a family being torn apart by a dream which had turned into a nightmare. He feared it was impossible to backtrack from the original contract.

James had arrived with a rehearsed smile. He was brash; he was in control. The all of a sudden he sobbed, "My life's falling apart and I don't know where it went wrong. I should be celebrating. I signed off the house today with Building Control and it's ready to move in. It was going to be the best day of my life."

I gave him a minute to recover. He picked up the story again and the reality began to spill out. It had been an all-consuming task. It had taken every moment of his evenings and weekends. To begin with, Monica had mucked in like a trooper and they'd left the kids to themselves, assuming they were fully occupied with homework and computer games. They'd have occasional rows just out of tiredness, but they blew over.

Slowly, imperceptibly, things started to change. They'd hardly had a meal together as a family; Monica was getting fed up with the unreliability of local tradesmen; the children became increasingly surly and uncommunicative. Eventually, when autumn arrived and the house was only half finished, Monica announced she wasn't going to spend another winter in the caravan. She was off to her sister's in West Haven, our neighbouring village, and she was taking the kids with her. At first James was glad to see the back of them. They were fed up with living on top of each other.

Then the phone calls started. They weren't so much a conversation as a one-way tirade from Monica about how the children were going wild. Eventually, from choice, Alicia and Rory came back to stay with some cousins in Kilfinan, though James gathered they were bunking off school regularly.

He realised he had become almost a recluse, even losing touch with his friends at St Finnan's. His life revolved around work from eight till six, then his construction project from seven till ten, plus all day Saturday and Sunday. Last year's weather had been wretched – highest rainfall for thirty years – and the building had fallen well behind schedule. The second winter in the caravan had been the most miserable time of his life.

On the plus side, he was still in touch with Monica and she would even discuss things with him in a civilised way; and he had met both Alicia and Rory a few times in an internet café which passed as neutral territory. But their finances were a disaster. The whole project had been based on two incomes to keep on top of the loan. Now Monica was keeping her earnings to herself and he had to send money towards the children's upkeep.

Up to this point I had said hardly anything, just making intermittent noises of agreement to add to the non-verbals. When James eventually finished I was at a loss. If he had been telling me about the death of a relative or that he had contracted a serious illness, I would at least have had some training in what to say. But this was a real mess and I didn't know where to begin.

"I'm glad you came to see me," I said. It was mostly true, if a little hollow. Yet I was particularly interested in why he had come to see me rather than his bank manager or a marriage counsellor. I got the impression that, for him, this was a much a spiritual as a practical matter.

Really, I didn't know what to suggest. Fishing for something to say, I lamely offered to lend a hand with fitting out the house, though I didn't know where I'd find the time, and was relieved when he told me the final details were already under control. Fortunately, James reassured me that he wasn't looking for anything practical, he just needed to confide in someone who understood, from a hands-on point of view, what he'd been going through. He was beginning to feel better already.

As I saw him off, Penny came through to the hall. It was no surprise to me that she'd overheard everything. It didn't even surprise me to learn that she'd been keeping a weather eye on the family and had gathered through the grapevine that Monica was as much at the end of her tether as James. And it certainly didn't surprise me that she had a suggestion for a way forward.

"What we need to do, Sam," she said matter-of-factly, "is pray through the house. You know, when a new church is commissioned it never really feels right until it's had several months of prayer sedimented into it. The three of us should pray our way systematically through each room."

I was so struck by the simultaneous practicality and impracticality of the proposal that I knew she was right. So I texted James about it and got a surprisingly positive response almost immediately. The following evening we arrived at his house with an Indian takeaway and bottle of wine. The driveway itself was impressive enough. Inside the house was wonderful; every detail of the plan had come to fruition. We marvelled at what the views would look like in the daytime. But to James it was an empty shell. He didn't even want to choose carpets and curtains in case Monica moved back and they weren't to her taste. So here it would remain, stark and unloved.

Our meal was surprisingly convivial, sitting at makeshift dining furniture of up-ended packing crates. Then we set about each room in turn. I started in the lounge with the familiar words of Psalm 127:1: *Unless the Lord builds the house, the builders labour in vain.* It took us best part of an hour to say all that needed to be said, by which time James looked visibly moved and, I would say, actually serene.

But there was an elephant in the room, so to speak. Another, equally immediate, problem which we'd been trying to overlook. The impending arrival of an outside broadcast unit, replete with presenters who were renowned for probing into homeowners' personal lives as much as the nooks and crannies of their houses. They were never content until tears were flowing as freely as wine at Cana.

Could we persuade Monica, at least, to return for the filming and play at happy families? Penny said she'd have a go in the morning. She phoned James the following day with the news:

"Well, we had a good long talk, but I'm afraid it's no go. I think she'd like to be friends and is insatiably curious about the inside of the house. But she's not ready for the big reunion. And she couldn't keep up a charade in front of cameras. I agree with her on the last point – she'd crack under the interrogation."

James realised he'd been clutching at straws and thanked Penny for trying.

"But" she continued, "we can offer the next best thing. Sam and I can join you as the helpful neighbours."

It was better than nothing and James welcomed our support.

What neither I nor James had twigged was the amount of time Penny had spent dealing with the media in her former life. As marketing director she'd had plenty of experience at working with the company's press officer and dealing directly with journalists. She knew how to avoid giving them an inch.

However hard the presenters probed, however much they suspected, Penny deftly deflected them. She turned their questions round, steered them towards safe territory, and told them plainly when something was none of their business. At the end of the shoot, not a tear had been shed, nor had a single confidence been broken. It was a class act for which Penny received our fulsome praise.

After we'd gone, James had evidently had a long phone call with Monica and convinced her it would be a bad idea to see the house – her house, of course – for the first time on TV. She had eventually agreed to visit on condition that Penny and I would chaperone her. We could hardly back out now.

And so it was that we all got together in the new house. Everyone spent the evening treading on eggshells, but it was all very civil. As we popped Monica back at her flat Penny handed her a card. "Please read it" she said simply. "I'll call you in the morning." She'd shown me what she'd written beforehand to get my affirmation. *The wise woman builds her house...,*

Proverbs 14:1, it started, and then there were a few sentences about how the bible refers to a house not just as a building, but to all of the people, treasures and memories which it contains. Could they re-build all of that, putting in as much effort as went into the bricks and mortar? I had a similar word with James a couple of days later.

That was about three weeks ago, and there are no signs of a dramatic breakthrough yet. It's probably unrealistic to expect anything so quickly. But we both think it will happen. The children appear to be back on the rails after a short-lived adolescent rebellion. Both parents at least want to be friends, and there's certainly a flame that hasn't gone out. And, after all, it is a fantastic house.

And James has started coming back to church. He tells me it was remarkably easy; that he's been accepted back into the old fellowship as if he'd hardly been away, and people have been thoughtful enough not to ask unnecessary questions. We've been in touch with Monica, who understandably still feels emotionally vulnerable and wary, but tells us that our friendship has helped to steady her faith.

We're not going to pretend that re-building will be simple, but we do feel that they're starting from the right place. We'll stick with them on their journey and it will be good for us too. We know where we've neglected building our own house. Penny told me last night that she'd checked how many times the bible tells us not to be neglectful and gave up counting once she'd passed twenty.

So, tempting though it may be, I'm not going to covet James's house; or his wife, car, servants, animals or anything that's his. Sam, for all his experience in the world of construction, has plenty of house-building of his own to do.

7. JANETTE:

Caught Off Guard

Janette Wolf texted Penny one Friday.

She hadn't slept well the previous night. Insomnia was rarely a problem for her, and she was cross that her mind kept racing for no apparent reason. The more she tried to calm her thoughts and committed her restlessness to prayer, the more her head was invaded by unbidden thoughts. At the end of a working day, she was invariably dog tired and fell asleep with ease until, refreshed, she awoke five minutes before her seven o'clock alarm.

Work was Janette's life, yet she was also a diligent member of St Finnan's, often arriving early for a morning service to enjoy the tranquillity. She spoke to few people at the church, I suspect out of choice, having little – as she supposed – in common with them.

Penny pointed her out to me first. I had observed her casually, without really noting and naming her. But Penny instinctively identified her as a kindred spirit. No need to conform to traditional niceties. Purposeful and assured, successful without being arrogant, and a touch pietistic. Within a matter of weeks, Janette had enlisted Penny as her *anam cara*, her spiritual confidante. Yet Penny was surprised when she received a genuine *cri-de-coeur*.

Janette eschewed the term Superwoman, though she would have had more justification than most. She managed the client liaison team in Kilfinan call centre, the town's major employer since our little dockyard closed. She left her house at eight, having shepherded husband and children to work and school. At five, or as soon after as business permitted, she would return to cook a freshly defrosted meal from the batch she'd prepared over the weekend. This activity arose not from manic energy or self-martyr-dom, but from her ardent belief in family, and her lynchpin role in holding it together.

The Wolfs were a potentially dysfunctional unit. Margo and Becca were in their early teens, with adolescent rebellion in full spate. Quentin was affec-tionate and empathic, but as useful as the proverbial chocolate teapot when it came to organisation and discipline, qualities which their daughters exploited to maximum effect. His natural affability and social ease did, fortunately, help him earn a decent crust as a veterinary supplies salesman, and endear him as the Chair of St Finnan's pastoral visiting team. Indeed, he probably helped disproportionately to hold several other couples and families together. But it would have been a different story in his own family, which came as close to fissile as possible whilst still remain-ing nuclear, had it not been for Janette's cussedness in facing down disputes and organising whole-family activities.

It was not as if she had boundless energy or Solomon's judgement, and at times she would have been beyond her wits end had she not been able to turn to Penny. I never pried into the finer details of their friendship, but I suspect that Janette genuinely found Penny a source of spiritual inspiration, whilst Penny was curious to discern whether she did indeed have a latent gift for counselling. It was clear to me too that, whilst Penny had set her face to trying to settle into Kilfinan, she still relied heavily on initial acquaintances to stem her yearnings for the life she had left behind. Yet despite the imbalanced nature of the relationship, I'm sure it thrived on genuine affection and mutual admiration.

Despite a self-confessed fragility, Janette felt it important to be a champion of Christian values in both her domestic and working life, even when this entailed a stiff dose of self-sacrifice. With some justification, she saw her workplace as spiritually dark and she took seriously her responsibility to spread light. She was not overtly evangelical, but neither was her faith unobtrusive, and she hoped that her conduct and values might prove an effective witness to those around her.

One particular Thursday in July, Kilfinan was visited by an uncharacteristic anticyclone and a consequent heat and stuffiness in the offices. None of the buildings hereabouts benefited from air conditioning, which architects assumed to be a wasteful luxury at such latitudes.

Call centres are not the most conducive places to kind words at the best of times, and are particularly volatile on a stifling and oppressive summer day. People who normally get on well together can suddenly explode. A few ill-disguised asides about arriving late, not hitting targets, talking too much, talking too little or poaching clients can spark off confrontations which then fester beyond their natural shelf-life. To this, add all the usual emotional rollercoasters of a workplace populated with late teens and twenty-somethings, and you get an idea of the managerial and pastoral role of a team leader. None of this is helped when you have a line manager who demands nothing less than humanly unattainable performance levels – his constant boast was to have won 'telesales Person of the Year' two years running.

A call centre had not been Janette's anticipated career direction. However, with a modest degree from a mid-ranking university, returning to work in the middle of a recession after a career break, she was glad to be offered any sort of job with a modicum of seniority. Even in her late thirties, she found herself as the elder stateswoman of a young team, whose members she often perceived as irritatingly immature and uncommitted. In return they at least accorded her a degree of veneration befitting her antiquity and experience – despite her Palaeolithic outlook and ethical twinges about some of the call centre's business.

Janette had met Quentin at university when they had ended up sitting next to each other at an Alpha Course supper. Both had a slight inclination towards spiritual matters though neither had had a church upbringing; the Alpha Course had been a way of putting their toes in the water whilst making new friends in a strange and intimidating environment. Both had been convinced by the teachings and fellowship of the Alpha Course but, whilst Quentin teetered on the borderline of faith, Janette retained her initial fervour and believed firmly that God put people in places and situations for a reason. Whilst she found working at the call centre to be stressful and unimaginative, she accepted that this was where she could be brought into contact with numerous people with whom she could share God's love.

Thus, she made a point of arriving at the call centre early, to allow herself a time of prayer and reflection. Once the phones started ringing, she knew there would be little opportunity even for arrow prayers.

Some days are worse than others, and Thursday had shaped up to be one of the worst. Matt was late at his desk and she could hear his phone ringing. Intercepting it, she received a tirade of abuse from a very irate electricity customer. She could see the customer's point of view, over a threat of disconnection arising from an incorrect bill. She did her best to assuage him, though it took her several minutes to stem his stream of profanities and persuade him to accept an apology and a swift resolution of his grievance.

When Matt finally came in with excuses about a sick daughter she was blunt with him and referred sarcastically to the fact that she might actually have some family issues of her own to deal with. It was a fair point: the number of times she'd had to defuse early morning crises and still arrive on time with a can-do mindset. Matt barely had time to take his coat off before his phone started ringing again and another tongue lashing came down the headset.

Ten minutes later there was a lull and Janette dropped what she was doing to give them a heads-up for the day. They'd be starting a new contract to sell solar panels. This was coming on-stream with immediate effect and would have to be fitted into their present workload. But everyone would need to grin and bear it because it would provide continuity when the hamburger taste-panel contract expired.

It sometimes worried Janette to hear herself speak in such a manner, but she realised that this was the real world. Catering for customer preferences in a consumer oriented society was pivotal to success. It didn't matter whether the customer understood the problems of securing electricity supply; they paid the bills so were entitled to decent service. It didn't matter whether people obeyed the food police; food outlets should find ways of satisfying customer needs without causing long-term health issues. It didn't matter that people were pestered during their leisure time; there was a fair chance they were eligible to be compensated for some previously mis-sold insurance policy. Like it or not, call centres were the dynamos of the new regional economy.

And, like it or not, people have had to turn up unwillingly to work ever since there were serfs. So Janette couldn't afford to be sentimental. She had to turn up to work even if there was a family crisis. And she had to demand the same from her team. She treated them with fairness and equality. She put in a hard day's work, left personal issues outside the office door, and expected the same from colleagues. She took the flak from customers, absorbed criticism from her line managers in order to protect her staff, and privately gave her staff an ear-bashing in turn if they deserved it. It was the only way to keep their heads above water. Her attitude was non-negotiable and, by and large, her team respected her for it. She was fair, up-front and consistent, even if a bit of a religious nut.

Janette would give her team a full briefing on the new contract as soon as possible. It should have waited till the Monday morning meeting slot, but it was starting imminently and she'd have to juggle things sooner so that front-line staff were adequately briefed. The news was inconvenient and stressful, but nonetheless welcome.

She intercepted a call for Moira who'd had to dash for a comfort break, which should have been taken before she started work, but of course her bus was running late as usual and she'd only just reached her desk at one minute to nine. As Janette hung up Moira returned and said something about poor Matt's daughter with chickenpox, just as Donald, her line manager barked at her to come immediately to his office.

Donald wasn't pleased. He'd had the monthly sales figures and customer feedback. Was she aware how follow-ups on replacement kitchens were ten percent down on the previous month and the client was threatening not to renew the contract? Janette knew better than to answer that the previous month's figures were exceptionally high and that the project funding was time-limited anyway. Did she know her gas supplier's clients returned the third highest level of customer dissatisfaction amongst all their current contracts? Again, she knew better than to defend herself by saying that they'd accepted a contract from one of the country's less scrupulous utility companies.

The first time Donald had torn a strip off her she'd protested that it wasn't fair, and gave what she thought was a perfectly sound defence.

"No it isn't fair" came the caustic reply. "This is the real world. Don't expect it to be fair. Just do what you're paid to do and don't complain. We're playing a tough game."

Nowadays she simply looked Donald in the eye, thickened her skin, and promised she'd speak to the staff involved and show an improvement in next month's returns.

It was mid-morning when she got back to her desk. She bought her customary black coffee from the trolley – black because it didn't go cold so quickly whilst she was snatching intermittent gulps. She took a bigger gulp than temperature reasonably allowed, but the caffeine kick made up for the passing scald, and she blanked her mind whilst steeling herself for the next encounter.

Fortunately there was a momentary lull, and she called across to her team to update them on the flaying she'd just received from Donald. A minute suffced to convey the essence of his concerns and how they'd need to respond. She held up a hand when two of her staff started to ask questions or make comments. There would be time later. For now, the phones were ringing again.

The best thing about her job, Janette often said, was that time passed quickly. You never had a spare moment in which to get bored.

And soon it was lunch break. She sat in the faux leather bucket chair by the tinted window and pulled a low-fat sandwich from her bag. Half of her colleagues occupied other chairs; the other half either hadn't yet managed to extricate themselves from their posts or had gone outside for a smoke. She chatted about how the morning had gone, what they were planning for the weekend; but halfway through her sandwich her phone rang. She ignored it with a joke and continued nibbling cautiously. Then it rang again.

"I'd better answer it" she said.

"No, sit down. I'll take it", said Alex, her star teleworker. He intercepted the phone just ahead of her and, clutching the receiver with his shoulder and optimistically clinging onto a carbonated drink, sustained a one-sided conversation with an aggrieved customer. Janette retreated to her seat and bolted the remainder of her lunch before her half hour was up.

She was returning to her desk when a worried looking girl beseeched, "Can I have a word with you?"

"You're Joanne, the new intern, aren't you?"

"Mm mm," she nodded. "I was just hoping you could run me through the database again. I've been struggling this morning."

"Sorry, Joanne. You were shown yesterday. You'll have to find someone else or work your way through the online help. It isn't rocket science."

Actually, it wouldn't have taken Janette five minutes to refresh the intern's memory, but she adhered to the view that people need to get used to picking things up first time. Then she continued, "I can't have you being the weak link in our team." It was intended as a reaffirmation of the company's high professional standards, but elicited a crumpling of Joanne's crestfallen brow. The intern slunk forlornly back to her computer and stared helplessly at the screen before deciding that, as no-one was coming to her aid, she would have to resume the unequal struggle alone.

Returning to her desk Janette quickly brought herself up to speed on the incipient solar panels contract, and memorised the marketing pitch and stock responses to frequently asked questions. She needed immediate cover so that she could give her staff a briefing on it during working hours rather than make them stay on late yet again. It would be a stop-gap, but at least they would have learned the basics for when the phones started ringing in the morning, and then they could have a proper staff development session on Monday.

She strode over to where Clive, her opposite number on the online retailing team, was catching up with paperwork.

"Hey, Clive, I need you to help."

He finished something off, then looked up.

"I need you to give me cover for an hour so we can do a briefing on a new contract. It's coming in at short notice tomorrow morning."

"Get them to stay on after. You can see how busy we are. Sorry, Janette, can't help."

She started to get cross. Yes, she could see they were stretched, but surely he could do it if pressed.

"I'm sure you can, Clive. I can't ask my guys to stay on again. We've got homes to go to. And we'll have to spend the evening learning our new spiel. Come on. You want me to put in a good word for you on Monday don't you?"

They exchanged more sharp words but eventually she faced him down.

"Okay, I'll give you half an hour."

Clive instructed half his team to switch desks and work from the scripts that were placed in front of them.

Janette could see the pressure they were under but ignored the glares from Clive's reluctant conscripts. She gathered her thoughts for the briefing. Half an hour was just enough, then it was back to business.

At five her staff drifted away one-by-one. Janette stayed on another quarter hour to tie up loose ends and ensure a smooth transition to the evening shift. She finally logged off, stared briefly into the horizon, psyched herself up and headed for the car park.

Kilfinan had the merest apology of a rush hour and Janette was home in ten minutes. She pulled up alongside Quentin and the girls in the driveway and as she got out was instantly reminded about Becca's dance class in a hour's time. It had gone completely out of her mind. Still, not a problem. A little under an hour later everyone was changed, fed and watered, and the pair headed to the sports centre. It was a chance to relax with a book for an hour, though Janette couldn't concentrate and only managed a handful of pages. Something was nagging at the back of her mind. Nothing specific, not even a whirr of thoughts, just a feeling that something was needing to be dealt with.

That something continued through the night. Sleep wasn't normally a problem but this night she was fitful and she slept only in snatches. Somewhere in the small hours she was awoken by a dream; there was a sickly child and a man without a face was trying to calm it only he couldn't because there was a phalanx of phones that kept ringing and ringing. People started swirling and they were pointing their fingers at someone who could have only been her, but just as they were about to say something important she woke up. She tried to control her breathing and turned on her side, trying not to disturb Quentin. Sleep felt as if it would never return but it must have done because she woke suddenly from another dream where the intern was sitting in the rest area and her lunch was turning into insects and she was getting more and more terrified and was just about to say something when Janette again woke with a start.

She realised that the reason for this awakening was the inmates of the nearby poultry farm bursting into life. A cockerel orchestrated an avian symphony which was normally inaudible, but which on a cold morning carried clearly. She checked her alarm, though it was scarcely necessary to confirm that the hubbub meant it was five o'clock. An hour and a half later, she dragged herself up and stumbled bleary eyed and ragged into the morning routine.

Two strong coffees and a shouting match later she kissed Quentin goodbye and taxied the girls to school in near silence. Time to flip into work mode. She straightened her suit, checked her hair in the rear-view mirror, focused her mind and strode confidently towards the office. She didn't feel like doing her quiet time and couldn't focus her prayers, but she had a well-honed ritual to cope with such situations and they worked as ever. The notes for the day started with Proverbs 15:1, *A gentle answer turns away wrath, But a harsh word stirs up anger.*

The trickle of incoming staff swelled to a surge as the clock approached nine and, to her relief, no-one was late. She greeted them as cheerfully as her jangling nerves would allow, but the replies seemed cool and she attributed this as a response to her sleep-deprived terseness. Either that or it was Friday and people just wanted to get the day over and done with as soon as possible. She'd remembered to ask Matt about the baby and he grunted that everything was okay now; she said hi to Joanne who appeared to have a reassuringly normal packed lunch in her carrier bag. The team were quickly at work, without the usual banter or time-wasting, which she felt was no bad thing.

Even before it was ten, Donald had called her in for the regulation ear-bashing. It was the only management style he knew and she had accustomed herself to it. She managed to convince him that response times were only slower because of having to slot in the new contract with no additional staff, and she did appreciate that a little overtime next week would sort out the problem once everyone was up-to-speed on their scripts.

As she was starting the mid-afternoon Friday wind down, Alex came in and commented, "you weren't Ms Popular yesterday." It was said in a semi-jocular way, but it knocked her off balance. Janette looked at him confrontationally.

"Your ears must've been burning," he continued.

She took it from Alex. He had the fewest agendas of anyone in the office. He wasn't exactly Mr Nice Guy, but then neither would he play mind games; you always knew where you stood with him.

Janette fixed her eyes in a way that beckoned him to continue.

"Matt's kid was really bad; had to go into hospital you know. Matt busted a gut to get into here as soon as he could, leaving his partner in tears. The intern was in tears later, too. To be honest, I'm worried about her – she seems to take things very personally. You might have given her the kid gloves treatment. And Clive's staff were fizzing about covering for you – as if they didn't have enough on their plates."

"Oh come on" said Janette. "That's unfair. I was run ragged yesterday. It's not too much to ask other people to pull their weight".

"Whoa, whoa, whoa," Alex said. "I'm not accusing you. I'm just letting you know they were badmouthing you whilst you were out. It may not be fair that they're cross with you, but that's how it is. Don't worry. It'll all blow over when you buy them a drink this evening."

Janette was whacked and she wanted to see the family. She hadn't been planning to head down to the bar after work. But on this occasion perhaps it would be a good idea. The reason she hadn't reacted more strongly to Alex was that the dreams were still niggling. It was as if he had said the words which the characters in the dream hadn't been able to speak. Had she really disowned her colleagues three times?

At 4.30, Janette ducked out of the office, switched on her mobile and left a message for Quentin that she'd be back by seven. Something had cropped up and she needed to buy her wonderful team a drink. She left a message for Penny – "cock crowed for me this morning, can u do Harbour Lights at 3 tmrw?" Then she silenced her mobile, returned to the office and said:

"Hey, guys. It's been a tough week. Let me buy you a round at The Tavern."

They gladly acquiesced, and after a drink everyone seemed to be friends again.

But Janette still needed to talk it through with her *anam cara* the following afternoon.

Penny listened patiently, and smiled sympathetically when Janette concluded, "You see, I realise now that all the time I'm at work I'm a witness. My dreams were telling me I'd denied Christ three times. Unwittingly of course, but I was caught off guard."

"Let me get you another coffee. A decaf of course or you won't be sleeping again". They laughed.

Penny has become a seriously good at giving a sympathetic hearing, and offering wise counsel without sugaring the pill. So she gently nudged Janette into agreeing that, as a Christian, you're never off duty. People judge you by unreasonable standards. They expect you to have the patience of Job and the wisdom of Solomon, or else they dismiss you as a hypocrite.

"That's the real nub," she suggested. "It isn't fair really is it? It never has been. We just need to remind ourselves of the saints who went before us. Life was rarely fair for them, either, but they grew to live with that. And, in the long run, people ended up admiring them and realising they had something special."

Janette smiled knowingly. She knew that people were indeed always watching her to see if she slipped from her pedestal. She knew they were always eager to criticise her for the least thing that might be considered unchristian. But she knew, too, that they respected her for trying hard, and for standing firm on matters of ethics and values. They knew where she stood, that she gave it her best shot, that she cared for them. Janette took another sip of coffee, paused for a moment, then said, "No, it isn't fair, but it's the real world. We're playing a tough game."

"Spoken like a true saint", Penny grinned.

8. RACHEL:

Daylight Peeps Through

Ross hurried on towards school, his head down, looking away from me.

He'd always been a friendly lad, a regular attender at our youth fellowship until last year, but I suppose at 16 it's uncool to acknowledge grown-ups, especially those of a religious ilk. Still, I was surprised not even to get a grudging glance from him. His parents both worked in some capacity in education, though their days of actual teaching were well behind them, and their vestigial faith led to them attend St Finnan's only on high days and holy days.

I pondered a moment at Ross's manner because it somehow seemed deeper than mere aloofness but then, having preoccupations of my own, pressed onwards to work. I realised that I, too, must have often unwittingly ignored acquaintances. Perhaps Ross had been no more than absent-minded; I thought no more of it.

That evening, however, we had a call from Rachel Greig, a near neighbour who had once referred to herself as an ex-attender at St Finnan's. I smiled in pleasant surprise on seeing her at the door, but she looked distracted and rather peremptorily asked if she could speak to Penny. Unfortunately my wife was trying to sleep off a headache and wouldn't take kindly to being disturbed. I asked Rachel to come inside whilst I went upstairs.

Penny made her irritation clear when I tiptoed into the darkened room. "Rachel Greig's here," I said. "She'd like a word with you."

Penny thought for a moment but looked none the wiser. "Dark haired, tall, fortyish. Helps out at a charity shop. Has a son called Gavin in the Youth Club and a younger daughter in the Guides." I checked my notebook. "Yes, Sophie. Age 13."

Penny was still struggling.

"Best friends with Annie Bell. Had a bookstall at the Easter Fair."

Recognition dawned. Headache, rather than memory, was the problem.

"What does she want?" came the groggy reply.

"Wouldn't say, but it's you she'd like to see."

"Okay. Show her into the study. I'll be down in five."

Penny came down looking fresh as a daisy, as if she had been looking forward to the visit all day.

"Hi Rachel. Thanks for dropping by. Would you prefer coffee or tea?"

If Rachel had been asked if she wanted a drink, she'd have declined. All she wanted was to talk, with the minimum of delay. But by now Penny had twigged that if she wanted to put a confidante at ease, it was best to do so with mug in hand. After a few moments' delay Rachel replied, as if suddenly fathoming the question, "Oh, er, a decaf please".

"I'll leave you to it," I whispered, and busied myself in the study. Half an hour later I heard voices in the hall, followed by the sound of Rachel getting into her car. I was about to go down, when I heard Penny ascending the stairs.

"Well, that's a tough one," she began. "She has it on good advice that someone in Gavin's year is selling drugs."

My immediate instinct was to back off. This sounded like deep water. Something for the police. Not something we should get involved in.

"How reliable is the source?"

"Well, the source is Gavin, though he hasn't actually been offered anything directly. He's certain it's going on and is pretty sure he knows the culprit. And he reckons it isn't just a few 'legal highs' either."

"But no actual hard evidence?"

"No. But Rachel was sure he was telling the truth. She'd asked Sophie about it and got a similar story in which the same name cropped up."

"Why did she want to speak to you?" I asked. "Why not just go straight to the teachers or the police?"

"I'm not certain. Perhaps she just trusts me. People are starting to turn to me. Don't know why."

"Perhaps you're beginning to find your true vocation," I suggested.

Penny paused quizzically, then returned to the matter in hand.

"Gavin was scared of the boy in question and didn't want to be implicated."

"Did Rachel name the suspect?"

She nodded.

"Can you tell me?"

She hesitated, then added that she'd promised confidentiality.

"If I mention a name, could you confirm whether that's the person?"

She nodded.

"Ross Miller?"

"No", she said quickly, but added, "though his name was mentioned. I think he's involved in some way."

"Does Rachel want us to do anything? I mean, it's not really something we should be involved in. What does the rest of her family feel about it?"

"Oh, well, they've discussed it. She mentioned that her husband was happy for her to speak to us. How had he described us? 'Wise and discreet', I think."

It was nice to know that we were becoming trusted by the locals, even if it didn't help me decide what to do next.

"The school should have a drugs policy," I suggested. "That would be a good starting point. Let's check their website."

It took a degree of sleuthing, but eventually we located the policy.

There was the usual stuff about a drugs-related curriculum. There was also a commitment to appointing a governor with a lead role. It affirmed the total unacceptability of supplying illegal and unauthorised drugs on school premises, but also pussyfooted around threats of punishment, instead emphasising a primary concern for health and safety. The head teacher would be likely to interview pupils about a drug related incident. But this would only be with the intention of confirming or rejecting suspicions; actual investigation would be a police matter. Parents of pupils would be informed, along with a variety of external agencies.

It was less clear what might happen where there were mere rumours, or where a student or parent had made an allegation.

Penny and I were rather relieved to discover that the culprit needn't necessarily get into trouble with the law unless a police officer actually found drugs on a pupil. In most other circumstances, the school's policy indicated a range of responses from the punitive to the pastoral. In fact, the school didn't have a legal obligation to report an incident to the police and could deal with many cases through internal procedures.

We were reassured to find that the policy was not too draconian. Much as we detested the peddling of drugs amongst schoolchildren, we didn't like to see insecure and confused adolescents stigmatised with a criminal record. Of course, if there was a drugs problem at the school, we should do what we could to nip it in the bud. But how to do it without blundering amateurishly into an unknown territory?

The policy stipulated that ultimate responsibility for a response lay with the Headteacher. This was patently obvious, but also perhaps the basic cause of my anxiety and uncertainty. The new incumbent was an ambitious chap, Mark Tennent, who made no secret of his dislike for the church. The Episcopals, along with our neighbouring ministry teams, had tried in vain to get a Christian input into school assemblies but Tennent would have none of it. He wouldn't even let in the Gideons to distribute free bibles. So how could Penny and I, as people without children at the school, who were conveying mere hearsay, and with a voluntary church status as our only credential, reasonably speak to him?

It was a delicate and complex matter which we devoutly wished was someone else's problem. But at the same time we were pleased that someone should turn to the church for support and guidance. Eventually, we agreed that the initial course should be to raise the matter with Max and hoped he would absolve us of the need to take further action. I rang the rectory, earnestly hoping that Max would invite me to leave it in his capable and experienced hands.

Little could have been further from the truth. I was careful not to mention any names or indicate any identifiable details, and gave him only the most generalised sketch. Max umm-ed and ah-ed in the right places and all the time sounded as if he was going to make some profound observation, but ultimately all he said was, "Well I'm sure you can handle this one admirably as usual Sam. You're a man of the world. Thanks for sharing it with me and let me know how you get on."

I suppose the natural course of action would have been to raise the matter with the relevant governor but, not to put too fine a point on it, the governor in question was well known to us as someone pathologically incapable of keeping a secret. Raising a confidential matter with him would have been as effective as placing a block advertisement in the Kilfinan Gazette. A direct approach to the headteacher seemed inevitable. Penny phoned Rachel to ask whether she'd mind, and the latter was only reluctantly assuaged by Penny's assurances about confidentiality.

It was getting late and there would be no chance in the morning to phone the school before heading to work, so I shot off an email to the school secretary requesting a meeting with the Head on a matter of some urgency. I wasn't too hopeful of the outcome so was pleasantly surprised when I checked my Inbox on arrival at work and found a reply saying that Tennent hoped I could meet him in his office at one o'clock, that very day.

Given that it was Lent, I could feel virtuous both about skipping lunch and going into the lion's den, without my absence from work being noticed.

I approached Tennent's office with a degree of trepidation, even though I'd rehearsed my words many times. As it turned out, I was pleasantly surprised by his demeanour. He had a brisk and business-like style and his eyes were as forthright as they were intelligent. With a firm handshake, he bade me sit in an armchair. I briefly introduced myself as an engineer and lay reader and he conveyed interest in both. Though he gave me his undivided attention, he was evidently busy and I was invading his break, so I cut to the chase.

"I know you're very concerned about the pastoral needs of your pupils, so I felt I ought to tell you that I suspect a drugs-related incident has occurred on school premises."

He raised his eyebrows in a gesture of concern rather than surprise.

"I don't want to breach confidences," I continued, "but a family friend spoke to us last night that her children both suspected a fellow pupil of supplying illegal substances. It's only second hand, of course, but I have every reason to suppose it's true."

"And why didn't your friend come to see me themselves?"

"I suppose they felt they would be putting their children at risk. From what I gather, things would be very unpleasant for them if they were traced as the source of the report. And I suppose they felt that I had some sort of standing on pastoral issues."

He bore none of the anticipated disdain towards my pastoral credentials. He betrayed nothing other than thoughtful concentration.

"Can you tell me who the children are? It would be more effective if I could speak to them myself."

"Sorry, but I've promised confidentiality."

He didn't press the matter, and I sensed he recognised that a man of the church had to keep his word.

"However," I continued in order to break the awkward hiatus, "I do have a name I could mention. There's a pupil whom I think it would be worth speaking to. I want to stress that I don't think he's involved in any way, in fact he may be a victim rather than a culprit, but I wonder if you might have a gentle word with him. It's Ross Miller."

"Hm. Not one I would have suspected to be caught up in this sort of thing," Tennent replied in a way that conveyed he had an instant recall of all the school's eight hundred or so students.

"And probably he isn't. So please go gently on him," I added. "But I'm pretty certain something's bothering him and I think it may be related to drugs."

"Well, thank you for coming to see me, Mr Waite. I take this sort of thing with the utmost seriousness and will definitely act. Though of course I'll treat the Miller boy with kid gloves as you suggest."

As I was leaving, he added, "What branch of engineering did you say you were in?"

"Structural, actually."

"Interesting. I might come back to you on that one."

I felt rather pleased that the meeting had gone so well and that I'd been treated without the patronising tone that I usually get from anti-church people. Or, for that matter, the obsequious tone which I often get from pro-church people.

Both Penny and the Greigs shared my optimism and this turned out to be well founded. I had a message from the school secretary a couple of days later saying that the Head would like to meet me again at my earliest convenience.

Skipping another lunch gave me a glorious sense of smugness. Tennent told me how he had called Ross to his office shortly after our meeting and had

had a firm but fair talk. The boy had evidently broken down as soon as the matter was raised. It seemed a relief for him to talk about it and he had tearfully confessed to buying some tablets on one occasion and then being bullied, both physically and via text, to buy more, which he couldn't afford and didn't want. Tennent had gone out of his way to stress that the school was more concerned about his welfare than about punishing him, and how commendable it had been that he hadn't tried to cover up. But he needed to know who was behind the offences, and the school would deal with it in a way that didn't involve the culprits knowing the source of information.

It emerged that there was a nucleus of gang members, whose membership came as a surprise to no-one. Tennent had called them to his office individually, warning them of the gravity of the situation and, one by one, details emerged which gave a clear indication of activity and guilt.

He had decided it needed to be a police matter, despite the adverse publicity for the school. Far worse might happen unless a matter of such seriousness was dealt with swiftly and authoritatively.

Later on, he thanked me effusively for my efforts. And then, he surprised me by asking me to give a talk in their Careers Guidance series. He was keen to encourage more pupils to take up engineering.

It's a long time since I've attempted to speak to teenagers, certainly *en masse*, and the experience swelled my admiration for teachers. But I think my talk went down rather well, so well in fact that it seems likely to become a regular fixture. And I should add that Ross Miller is now planning to study engineering at Strathclyde University.

What surprised me even more was that Tennent invited me to join a small panel to devise a set of materials for use in school assemblies. This was something to which I felt unsuited and needed to check with the local clergy that I wasn't usurping their roles. But they welcomed my invitation gleefully and I must say it has proved more enjoyable than I'd imagined.

The content was totally different to when I was a pupil – neither a hymn nor a bible reading in sight. Nor was there another person of faith on the panel, though they all had consciences and some jolly good ideas. I'm still not even at first base yet in terms of evangelising, but there are chinks opening up here and there; little bits where the Light gets in.

As you might expect, I chatted about the matter with Ellie after Eucharist one Sunday and was pleased that for once I had a conversational gambit that was genuinely newsworthy. A church input to the Academy's pastoral programme, no less. She expressed enthusiasm in the way the school had reacted to my intervention and, rather less expectedly, also admitted to regret at her own school's lack of career guidance on engineering. Yet, she didn't seem at all surprised that a doorway had opened up for me.

"You know, we have a saying in these parts, Sam – that 'daylicht will peep throu a smaa hole'." She paused to scrutinise the expression of bafflement on my face. And then we both smiled together as the translation eventually sank in.

9. ARCHIE:

A Blessing In Disguise

I realise I am unrealistic in my expectations about churchgoers… I expect them all to be easy-going, successful, confident, talented and resilient. Of course, I'm usually disappointed, but the problem is mine, not the church's. People aren't like that. Go into any walk of life – any club, any workplace – and you find the hotheads, the misfits, the moaners, the screamers, the serial best friends and the conspiracy theorists. Congregations can seem almost tame by comparison.

But Archie was hard-going. Probably not hard-going by the standards of the ancient church. I have an impression that, over the centuries, churches and orders have embraced people with severe disabilities and behavioural problems who were just part of the warp and weft of daily life. People who were too much for their families to look after and who stood little chance of fending for themselves.

Even so, when people like Archie need the loving support of our congregation, it's a big ask.

I hadn't known Archie before the accident. By all accounts he had been a charismatic professional. Something to do with creative design, I think. His children, Fraser and Rona, had both recently graduated and he and Eve were enjoying being empty nesters.

Archie, for the first time since his postgraduate days, was finding time to do some serious walking at weekends. And that was when the accident happened. I've never found out the precise details, but it appears that he was undertaking a traverse in the Cuillins when a snowpack gave way and he fell about 100 metres. He was airlifted to Raigmore Hospital in Inverness where they patched him up but he has never functioned properly since.

He'd hoped to return to work, but it quickly became obvious that this wouldn't be possible. Not only was he half crippled, but his memory was impaired and his personality had changed. His social skills were lost. He couldn't control anger and flew off the handle at the slightest provocation. Eve, who surely possesses the patience of a saint, bore the brunt of it. But he soon became a burden, almost an embarrassment, to St Finnan's.

Fortunately, he had the capacity to remain mostly silent during sermons and liturgy, but his out-of-tune singing and inappropriate alleluias during prayers put Max and me dreadfully on edge during services. His tendency to grasp the wrists of people whom he hardly knew, and prevail on them to run him an errand, was disquieting. He demanded to be chauffeured to church and required a minder throughout. Eve was at the end of her tether, and on Sundays relied on the church taking over, which in turn placed recurrent demands on a small nucleus in our congregation.

In honesty, few of us would have been saddened if Archie had stopped attending. Nor did we give much thought to Eve; indeed, I barely recognised her because all this had preceded our arrival. We had unsuccessfully tried to persuade Archie to take the Council's flexi-bus service to church, which would have transported him almost door to door, but he treated our suggestion with contempt. On the occasions when it was my turn to be his taxi, I often leaned on Penny to do the honours, even though I knew she couldn't abide him.

One bleak and dreary January Sunday, the time of year when the sun is at its most miserly and when people cling on grimly for their next wage packet, I heard that Eve was ill. Not seriously ill, just a rather virulent strain of 'flu, but she was confined to bed and couldn't look after Archie. She needed to rest and get better for her part-time job at the cottage hospital – her income was their principal means of survival, given the insufficiency of their carer's allowance. I had managed to avoid greater involvement since our arrival last year, but on this occasion felt duty bound to invite Archie to our house for Sunday lunch, permitting Eve to starve her way to recovery.

At the end of the service I waited for Max to finish the blessing and, after a few moments of peace and reflection, walked towards the door to chat with worshippers. But Archie commandeered me en route.

"Sam, Sam" he called stridently. "Here, now!" And then, in a piercing voice, "Get me a tea and biscuit. I've been waiting for you lot to shut up. Get a move on, chum!"

I waved at a group of regulars heading towards the door and they exchanged a knowing smile. Then I helped Archie to his feet as, with his free arm, he pushed the bystanders out of the way and with a surprising degree of strength yanked me in the direction of the annexe. I was struck by his single minded pursuit, which brooked no obstruction, as much as by his smell and roughness. When we arrived at the refreshments table he barked his orders at the ladies of our delightfully loyal catering group, who humoured him with good grace.

We shuffled back across the hall and towards the main door, as Archie shouted greetings to various people whom he considered as 'best mates'. He was heavy, stubbly and boorish, but I filtered out these aspects as I struggled to maintain balance and momentum. Eventually we made the front door and Penny came to our assistance.

She said, "Hi Archie" in a reluctant sort of way without reciprocating his gesture for a kiss and embrace. Instead, she backed off and volunteered to bring the car round. In a couple of minutes she reappeared and I managed to lever Archie into the front passenger seat whilst I squeezed into the back.

As we drove off, Archie immediately launched into a sustained gripe about the past week and how bored he'd been, how his niece had only been round once to read the paper to him, how he'd had a couple of falls, and how he got bored listening to the rubbish on the radio. He resented the time when Eve was out at work and, by the time she got back, he was desperate for tea, coffee, food and general daily necessities.

I ushered him into the house and he looked round, commenting on how much better it was than his own home and how he'd like to invite himself round several times a week. I settled him into the comfiest armchair; he sank awkwardly and uncomfortably, or at least his habitual expression conveyed it as painful. He kept exchanging glances between me and his watch, giving the unspoken impression that Penny was spending too long in the kitchen when he expected to be having lunch. He wasn't much company, but then I knew in my heart that he didn't have much of a life. His hitherto sharp mind was now befuddled by analgesics and mood swings, and by incessant pain from his reluctant limbs and joints.

Still, I could understand Penny's coolness when he suddenly yelled through to see how lunch was doing because he was hungry. Plus how she felt after placing an excellent chicken casserole before us, when he instantly commented that it wasn't as good as the Saturday roast produced by his sister.

We did our best to chat to Archie for an hour or so after dinner, our rather one-sided conversation punctuated by requests for the toilet and other necessities. However, we exchanged knowing glances as it approached the pre-agreed time when we might reasonably return him to Eve.

With some difficulty, given that he was now clearly enjoying this new environment, we persuaded him that it was time to return home. We drove to his house, where a bleary eyed Eve welcomed us at the door and thanked us profusely with a smile that peeked through from a grey face. We helped Archie down the vestibule and ushered him to the sitting room.

We couldn't help but gaze around. This little semi was the home of two professionally qualified graduates who had been on promising career tracks, but now it was threadbare and neglected. The carpets were thin and clashing, the paint mildewed, the curtains faded, the furniture mean, and the kitchen a clutter of unwashed dishes. Eve looked drawn, yet mortifyingly grateful for the few hours' respite we'd given her.

I would have stayed to chat but she didn't look up to it. Interestingly, there were still plaques with bible verses hanging on the wall and a small collection of spiritual books on a shelf. It looked as if faith was still important to Eve, even if we hadn't seen her at church for an age.

Penny asked if we could make them a cup of tea but Eve declined, gesturing that she'd prefer us not to go into the kitchen, so we quietly made our exit.

After we'd got home, I recall that Penny and I did little more than stare at each other for quarter of an hour. When we finally started to talk about the experience, we acknowledged our profound gratitude that we didn't have any such burden to carry, yet equally were aware that something similar could strike us at any time. What if I had a stroke and became totally dependent and demanding on Penny? What if she had a car accident and became reliant on me? What if one of our children had been severely autistic? Could we cope? Would we find ourselves isolated and marginalised? Would our faith hold up?

What could or should we be doing, we asked ourselves. Could our church, small and overstretched as it was, realistically offer regular support to people like Eve and Archie? These questions were hardly new. We recalled that God has chosen the foolish things of the world to shame the wise, and the weak things of the world to shame the strong. We remembered how David took in Saul's crippled grandson as an act of kindness. And we thought about the ways in which the law of Moses and the conduct of the early church in Jerusalem had prioritised concern for the indigent.

It was clear that Archie should be a blessing to us rather than a burden. It was apparent to us that we should try to bring a bit more respite and joy into Eve's life. But if we were to do this for one person, how could we do it for everyone? Our limited cadre of fit and healthy people would be overwhelmed if they tried to respond adequately to every needy situation in the congregation, let alone the wider community.

I recall we both simultaneously landed on the idea of inviting Eve round for coffee. It wouldn't do any harm just to chat to her about see if she had any suggestions. Choosing a moment when we knew she wouldn't be at work, Penny phoned and fortunately it was Eve rather than Archie who answered. She jumped at the chance for an outing, saying that Archie was happy to be left to his own devices for a while. She insisted on walking round to our house, even though it was over a mile, as the fresh air would do her good.

It was a beautifully mild afternoon when she arrived and she wore an almost ethereal smile at the delight of strolling through our quiet, panoramic lanes. The garden was alive with birdsong as we settled in the conservatory and I brought over a tray of tea and cakes. Eve wasn't the defeated, exhausted working-wife-cum-carer that I'd expected. She seemed remarkably content, someone who had willingly embraced the "for better, for worse" principle.

I don't know what we'd expected out of our meeting, but perhaps we'd secretly been hoping that Eve would assure us that everything was under control, that she was coping admirably and receiving lots of help from her family, and that she was more than grateful for what St Finnan's was already doing. But, although this was primarily a social and friendship visit, we also wanted to create space to discuss her hopes and fears. Her enforced confinement was a loss to the church, and we would have loved her to be able to attend St Finnan's regularly.

When Penny asked her about the pressures of caring, Eve thought for an awkwardly long time. She had a dreamy way with her, but also an attitude of depth and thoughtfulness. Choosing her words carefully, she suddenly said:

"I've been doing it so long that I hardly notice. Everything's become a routine. But, no, I don't have a life of my own. I have a carer's allowance but it doesn't go much beyond getting a cleaner in a couple of times a week and having someone come in for Archie at lunchtimes when I'm working. Fortunately Archie had an insurance policy at the time of the accident, and that went a long way towards paying off the mortgage, otherwise we couldn't make ends meet. I work three days a week for the cottage hospital, as I think you know, which is tiring to be honest, but at least it's a job. We've been far too under-staffed over the past couple of years and we're always under pressure. So, not great."

We nodded and gestured but didn't say much. We wanted to give her space. Gradually she opened up.

"Yes, it's a struggle. It wouldn't be so bad if Archie was more bearable. But he's on at me every minute. He can't help it, of course. But he never leaves me in peace, and nothing's ever done quickly enough or well enough."

Eve rattled on for a few minutes then suddenly checked herself and apologised for moaning, as if this was out of character.

"No, thank you for being open with us," I replied, and Penny nodded reassuringly. We asked if there was anything we could do to help. Eve thought hard, and again there were awkward silences, but eventually she said there was nothing she could think of. She was confident she'd got all the state assistance she was entitled to and she got occasional help from various relatives. She accepted the full consequences of her wedding vows, and this was all part of the deal. She was grateful to St Finnan's for giving space to Archie on Sunday mornings. Penny and I exchanged a guilty look over our grudging support.

We changed the topic to her spiritual life. Was she getting any contact with other Christians? Would she like to attend services or be involved in other church groups? Again, she thought longer and more deeply than we had expected. She seemed to be struggling emotionally. Even saints have their limits. Eventually, choking back tears but in such a stoic way that you would hardly notice, she confessed how she missed the support of home groups, the joy of singing. It had been such a long time that she had almost forgotten. She admitted she had allowed herself to get into a rut and had succumbed to tiredness and routine.

We chatted a while longer, and then she felt the need to get back to Archie. It was clear that whilst she was just about coping, her quality of life could be so much better with a little more input from St Finnan's. Even helping her to obtain a modicum of social contact during the week would be a vast improvement. And it was good to hear directly from Eve – because you would never have guessed it otherwise – that Archie found a great blessing in our church. He loved the services, he loved the attention from his helpers, he loved the lunches at people's houses. We honestly hadn't realised we made such a difference to his existence.

To cut a long story short, we took our turn more actively on the rota for Archie. We couldn't invent any extra hours in the week, but we could re-prioritise some of them. We've invited Eve to our house group, which she manages at least a couple of times a month, and where she has made a close friendship with a young widow. It seems, too, that Eve realises she has spent enough time in her tunnel and is now regrouping her resources to emerge and do new things.

A big boon has been Eve's lack of self-pity. We gather that a little while ago she wasn't coping at all well, and even now is only just managing to put on a brave face. She has surprising physical and mental resilience, and in this respect is perhaps untypical.

And we've been able to help more than we had anticipated. There's been a whole raft of little things which have caused us no extra burden but which have brought quite disproportionate blessings to Eve – putting her on the prayer list, inviting her to house group, keeping her in the loop on church events, making sure Archie gets a regular lift and Sunday lunch. Fortunately his tastes in food have turned out to be quite basic, and one of Nick and Clare's pies proves to be more than satisfactory, absolving Penny from the need to endure unintended slights about her own cooking. Now that she has got the measure of Archie, she is far more comfortable with him and, in a strange sort of way, quite looks forward to his visits because these get us out of our Sunday lunchtime rut.

To my surprise, I also began to realise that Archie was far more tolerated at church than I'd realised. He always made Max and myself uneasy during services; we were always acutely aware of his inappropriate moments. But it appears that these were, indeed, just moments, and most of the time most of the people didn't think of him any differently to anyone else. Ellie was the first to chide me about this and, since then, several others have reinforced the point.

So, things are now working out quite well with Archie and Eve. But it might so easily not have been the case. Looking back on it, if we'd parachuted into the situation a year or two earlier, we'd have found Eve in a very different frame of mind and truly struggling. We'd have found it far harder to offer her anything other than platitudes. We might have even ended up driving her further away from the church. And if she'd been a less resilient and balanced person the story might have been different again. It has taught us a lot about God's timing and about not relying on pat answers. Space, prayer, vulnerability, risk and hospitality come into it, as ever. And, as we are learning more and more, the saintliest of people are often at the outer margins of the church.

And at a personal level, something else has come out of it, too. Penny has found herself drawn, albeit quite willingly, into the Churches Together Carers' Group. They were in need of organisational and marketing skills; and her talent for making a big contribution within a carefully ring-fenced quantum of time has come to the fore. To her surprise, she finds herself quite good at being a people-person, and many carers have commented on how valuable they find her practical and matter-of-fact manner.

Of course, she's perfectly clear that the Churches Together group can't do everything, and shouldn't even try to, or else the volunteers will end up in a worse state than the people they're meant to be helping. In the grand scheme of things, it can do relatively little; but, on occasion, this modicum of extra support may tip the scales between coping and not coping. And their newly launched newsletter reflects this very fact. Penny showed me the inaugural copy – they've called it *The Pennyweight*. And for once she didn't groan.

10. GEOFF:

A Song of Ascents

Geoff eyeballed me across the boardroom table. Ten of us were seated at carefully judged intervals, not for the moment speaking, just seeing who would blink first.

Eventually he conceded, "Okay, leave the Projects budget as it is". My nerve had held and my budget was intact for another year. Geoff would need to look to some other division to make his savings. His accountant's eyes menacingly scanned the other managers to seek out the likeliest victim. But my ordeal was over. I'd done my homework well, and could breathe again.

The meeting over, I retreated to the Gents, and found Geoff alongside me.

"Fancy climbing Beinn Bhreac on Saturday?" he asked.

It was an unexpected gambit, and hardly the most congenial of settings. He usually only spoke to me when haranguing my division for being above its expenditure limit or below its income target. I took a moment to gather my thoughts. I knew that Penny would be in Glasgow so, for once, I had a clear weekend.

"Sure. I'm up for it," I replied, still in decision-making mindset.

And in a trice I regretted letting myself in for a serious climb. I enjoy walking but mountains are not my forte. Our part of Lincolnshire was pretty much flat as a pancake, whereas several of Kilfinan's surrounding hills are Munros. At 919 metres, Beinn Bhreac – Ben Vreck in my Anglicised diction – just topped the magical three thousand feet in old currency.

We made our arrangements and it was only later that I wondered why, out of the blue, my old adversary had challenged me to a climb. Not just my adversary, but everyone's *bête noire* – though to be fair, I had come to realise after my first few months that he was just doing his job. He was born to accountancy; his mission in life was to subject every senior manager to a just measure of pain, and to achieve savings whenever and wherever possible.

Anyway, what was done was done. I dug out my walking boots and hoped for decent weather.

So, very early Saturday morning, I set out for his flat, which lies close to the start of the main ascent. By the time I got there I was already starting to feel sufficiently exercised. He invited me in and I was immediately struck by the parsimony of the accommodation. These were curiously Spartan and sterile quarters for someone of such seniority.

A solitary framed photograph on the mantelpiece showed a younger Geoff – though it took me a few moments to recognise him – in a family grouping.

He came through and saw me looking at it.

"Happier days," he said. "That's Elisabeth, and those are Robin and Cathy. Ten years ago."

The children looked just about school age. He'd never spoken about them and, indeed, it never occurred to me that he had a backstory. I could only envisage him as the archetypal accountant, besuited and bespectacled, inhabiting a world populated by graphs and figures. Even dressed for the hills, he bore a grey formality.

Anyway, we didn't dwell on the matter, though I detected a tinge of wistfulness and emptiness when he spoke of his estranged family. For the present, I was far too concerned about staying upright for the next six hours.

We set out on our trek with the dawn silhouetting the purple hills across the bay, and for a moment I didn't feel envious towards Penny still slumbering cosily.

We started through the conifer plantations that now surround the western perimeter of Kilfinan and for the first half hour benefited from the well made forestry track. Then we emerged onto the open moor and I got a sense of what lay before me. The ever deteriorating track stretched ominously upwards into the distance, cancelling out my appreciation of its spectacular views and sudden isolation.

By this stage, I had run out of small talk. I was happy to let Geoff waste valuable energy in explaining the surrounding scenery. I hadn't realised he had originally hoped to be a geologist, only having been persuaded by his practically-minded parents to train for a profession with more varied and remunerative career prospects. Thus I learned about magmatic intrusions, metamorphic aureoles and glacial erosion, whose lengthy explanation at least afforded me opportunities to conserve my breath.

Fortuitously, just as my knees were starting to assume the consistency of blancmange, Geoff suggested pausing for a refreshment break and produced a exceedingly welcome flask of tea and slab of chocolate. It was over our snack that I started to realise the purpose of our endeavour. I was already having to concentrate over my fatigue and listened to Geoff's account receptively, but passively.

From explaining the shape of an adjacent corrie, he segued seamlessly into a confession about the massive gap in his life since Elisabeth had walked out, taking the children and, in his version, filling them with poisonous gossip about him. By now, I was sufficiently experienced in listening to tales of failed relationships to realise the importance of not leaping to the defence of one party without hearing it from at least one other perspective. However, Geoff's tone wasn't excessively self-pitying and I was too intent on recovering my breath to do anything other than appear sympathetic.

Equally, Geoff clearly wasn't looking for instant reassurance. His mind was still on Beinn Bhreac. But then he did say something which surprised me.

"Sam, you're a man of the cloth, aren't you?"

It's a common misconception, but now didn't feel the right time to disabuse him.

He continued, "I'm looking to you for help. I don't like to admit it, but my life's devoid of spirit these days. I look at you and see someone living a full life."

Again, it was a flattering perception. I resisted the temptation to refute his use of rose-tinted spectacles about our domestic life. It was clear that he wanted an opportunity to talk about something spiritual, and that I was the only one who fitted the bill.

"Are you saying this because I'm a reader at St Finnan's?", I asked. It was a daft question, borne of breathlessness. Of course he was.

"Of course I am," he replied with a smile.

I recall replying with some platitude that we all had a God-shaped hole which needed to be filled. But it was an inept gambit, simply one that helped me to play for time whilst I recovered my composure. Geoff wasn't one for self-pity. He was a shrewd professional and a disconcertingly athletic walking companion. He wasn't a 'new man' who wanted a weepy and empathic chat about emotional angst. He spoke about his marriage breakdown in a measured and matter-of-fact way that lost none of its primal tragedy.

"What haunts me most is the extent to which I'd taken things for granted," he said. "It's a classic case of 'you don't know what you've got till it's gone'.

I was silent in a way that showed I was listening intently and giving him space. I've developed a way of looking and breathing that says, "Okay, this isn't embarrassing, I'm interested, no-one can hear us, you're safe to talk."

I caught his eyes in a way that gestured I was waiting for him to speak next.

"Until you've experienced it you don't know. The normality of life, of having family round about you; then suddenly they aren't."

"I can see where you're coming from. I remember the loss we felt when our children left for university. They developed their own interests and friends. We hardly saw them even during the vacations. It was a wrench." I realised this was an inadequate response as I said it, but the quickness of Geoff's reaction still shocked me. It wasn't bitter; just more heartfelt and intense than the words alone convey.

"Oh, Sam. It was much worse than that. Of course, kids leave, and you don't realise what it's going to be like till it happens. But that's usually only after a gradual transition. And even then, they sometimes boomerang back. But this all happened so quickly. It's like losing a limb, or worse – perhaps your sight. You take it for granted. Things that have happened day in day out suddenly stop. You don't quite believe it. You think you'll wake up one morning and everything will be back to normal. But it won't. There's a new normality and it isn't anything you'd wanted or even anticipated. It wasn't that everything was perfect before. It's more a case that you hadn't realised how imperfect everything would be after."

He carried on. And on. Much longer than I had expected from this algebraic man of few words.

"Do you think it's irretrievable?" I asked. I went on to tell him about instances of families who'd got back together. Or where couples had eventually moved on and found new relationships, new lives.

Geoff answered in a way that I hadn't anticipated, though perhaps I should've done because it was almost a carbon copy of something I'd once seen before.

"I've no interest in anything new. It wouldn't have been difficult to start internet dating. It wouldn't have been difficult to take a new job and start a new life somewhere else. In fact, I've been a bit of a mug not to take up other job offers. But it's not something new that I want. I want things as they used to be. I want the old routine".

It took me a while to work out a reply, and even then it felt inadequate.

"And why isn't that possible? It doesn't sound like Elisabeth's in a new relationship at the moment?"

"No, so far as I'm aware she isn't. In fact I gather she's finding work and looking after the children single-handedly to be far more of a struggle than she expected. That's what makes it worse. To think, she prefers that to what we used to have."

"And what about the children? Are they still in touch?" What sounded like a simple and innocent question was, in fact, a carefully chosen one. I had been faintly aware that there were tensions and barriers in his personal life; previous seemingly inconsequential corridor conversations now started to slot into place.

"I try to keep in touch by text. Just the occasional 'hi, how's it going?' Sometimes I get a civil response in return. I see them occasionally, but it's not like there was a divorce, like I get formal access rights. Elisabeth's absolutely poisoned them against me. Told them a whole pack of lies. I don't even know the half of it, but I suspect."

For the first time this most publicly unemotional of men trembled with anger.

"The kids think I was having an affair. They think I was controlling. They think I was mean. They think I wasn't interested in them. They think I deprived Elisabeth of affection. They think I was emotionally cruel. None of that is true. She's brainwashed them into hating me."

I'd never suspected this was how he felt. He was always so calm and measured at work. But like the mathematician he was, he managed to compact a universe of variables into a minimum of words.

I realised I was on thin ice. He thought I had spiritual and experiential insights which I simply didn't possess. One careless word could be disastrous. But I did sense, through my limited experience, something that had clearly escaped Geoff. I heard the warning bells of bitterness and unforgiveness chime in my ears.

"Okay, let me think about it," was the best I could do. We smiled and nodded in the direction of the upward path. It was time to resume our walk.

The path was now becoming much tougher. Geoff was a lot fitter than me and kept passing comments on the geology, the history, the incoming weather. I could offer little more than gasps as I tried to pretend that neither fitness nor age was an issue. Geoff's seamless transition to a different topic of conversation reinforced my suspicion that he had developed well honed defence mechanisms. I wanted to go deeper, but for the moment had little idea how.

I trudged onward. I wasn't in trouble and I'd make it to the top, but I needed to guard my breath and measure my pace. Even so, my thought processes continued whirring as if in overdrive.

"You know a lot about the hills," I commented at last. It was a pointless observation but it played for time.

"School geography," Geoff replied. "It's surprising what sticks. Even from that hell-hole. At least some of the teachers were bearable."

"Not the happiest days of your life, then?" I quipped. It was a silly thing to say, but it was all that came to mind in my mildly distressed state. What I hadn't anticipated was the anger that Geoff's brief response conveyed.

"No. They were horrid." He paused a moment as if in one of his darker reveries. Then he continued, "My parents thought it was for the best, of course. A school that would make a man of me. Anyway, it's a long time ago now. Life's moved on."

It was an exchange that lasted only a few seconds, but there was something about his voice which I can't explain; somehow it said that life hadn't moved on in the slightest.

"So it was a character-building school then?" I replied in a clumsy attempt at humorous irony.

Again, it was a throwaway comment entailing minimal physical and mental effort.

He thought hard and, though I suppose it was no longer than half a minute, it seemed an era. I feared I was going to have to intervene to change the subject back to something lighter.

"No, the school was okay really. It was the parents who were the problem. No, actually I shouldn't judge. They were the wartime generation, wanting something better for their children."

"Are they still alive?"

"No. Long gone now; over a decade."

What emerged over the next mile was that he was the oldest of the children, the one expected to continue the family line. His parents were ambitious, respectable; the children were to be honourable, successful. Alternative lifestyles, masculinities, feminities weren't on their radar. They weren't physically abusive; comparatively liberal in fact. But any expression of emotion was strictly controlled; affection was reserved for daughters, and even then only on a conditional basis which required moral rectitude in return. "I suppose you'd say they were judgemental. Yes, definitely. That's what you'd say."

I let him talk on; it was the easy option. In fairness, he didn't sound bitter or resentful. In fact he seemed to open up and relax whilst telling me. As I struggled with the increasingly steep, uneven, eroded path it was easier to go into listening mode. Eventually he stopped, I think not because he'd exhausted his story or decided to stem his invective, but because it was a conversational gambit that had run its course.

Finally we reached the summit. And what a view! Kilfinan looked like an anthill far below us, and the hills stretched from Perthshire to Ulster, an untamed massif intersected by an immensity of lochs and sea. I recovered my breath and gave my disquietingly weary limbs a quarter hour's respite. We scanned the horizon, commented on the landscape history and the slightly iffy weather blowing in from the south-west and decided there was time to eat our sandwiches before descending.

Our conversation from then was mainly about work matters, not least because he never asked me about how my church or domestic life was going. I would, if given the occasion, have commented on Penny's ill-disguised frustration at the lack of prospects in this backwater, but burdening my problems on other folk isn't my job.

It's often said that the descent is more difficult than the ascent, but I think that this is the view of fitter people than I; for me, the downward trek was a welcome respite and I was able to sustain an equal share in the conversation. By the time we'd reached the car park we had decided on new business models and confirmed the inherent viability of my budget in relation to the company's foreseeable project activity. This was a conversation that did me no harm at all – indeed it gave me a strong sense of arrival within our senior management team. But of course, in the present context, it was of no eternal consequence.

We returned to Geoff's flat and I stayed there half an hour explaining, as simply and palatably as possible, various meanings of forgiveness. I think

Geoff thought I was trying to convert him, but in reality I was giving my wobbly legs time to subside. In the end, I had at least opened his mind to the possibility that, whilst he felt aggrieved at not being forgiven, the root cause perhaps lay deeper in his need to forgive others. I dared to suggest that this was so difficult that it was only possible with divine support.

At least he didn't reject my advice out of hand. He humoured me in a way that suggested it was at least as good as any other advice he'd received, and he thanked me both for the companionship on the walk and for sharing my thoughts with him.

I returned home to find that Penny had arrived ahead of me. I asked her how her day had been but she responded with a minimum of information and asked what kind of walk we'd had. I said very little about the walk itself because I knew she actually had little interest in the acquired aesthetic of open moorland, and I read from her expression that she was more interested in Geoff than Beinn Bhreac.

I gave her a quick résumé of our ambulant conversation and she nodded, knowingly. She thought for a while, cocked her head, gave me her quizzical Mona Lisa smile. This wasn't feminine intuition at work; I could almost hear her cogs of logic whirring. When her comment finally came, it was almost anti-climactic.

"There's something deeper going on here, isn't there?"

I replied with understatement that I'd expected her to say something more conclusive. But it was evident that up till now we'd only scratched the surface of the real nature of the problem. I had expected her to take sides quickly, with a perceptive judgement that either Geoff was a heartless android or that Elisabeth was a manipulative Jezebel. I should have known better.

"I don't know yet. Pray about it," she said.

That was what continued to surprised me about Penny. She was the consummate professional, the self-assured executive, the liberal yet adventurous theologian, who would suddenly surrender to the vulnerability of prayer. I should have been well used to it by now, but it always came with an element of surprise.

So, to cut a long story short, we prayed over the family for a generous amount of time. Yet it all seemed like one way traffic – us haranguing God, without any illumination in return. It was only as we discussed it over dinner that an answer started to emerge. It dawned on us that there was a more fundamental cause – a critical chink in the armour the Author of Lies could exploit. Deep in Geoff's heart was his inability to forgive others, probably most of all his late parents, but perhaps others who had been complicit in the criticisms and emotional detachment of his childhood and adolescence. Perhaps this detachment had verged on cruelty.

As we discussed it, it became increasingly clear. I could see Penny's forensic mind picking over the details, whilst I muddled through to a similar conclusion. We both regretted our lack of competence in psychoanalysis and counselling, and realised that we trod on dangerous ground when trying to give advice on such matters. But we had the benefit of scripture and the Holy Spirit, as Penny was always quick to remind me.

Progressively it all started to become clear. Geoff had a barrier of unforgiveness towards people who had controlled his early life. This led to an emotional coldness which he didn't perceive and probably rationalised as normality. Elisabeth had reacted to this insensitively in a rather selfish way, but one which was perfectly within the bounds of normal human frailty. She had concluded that the grass would be greener on the other side of the fence. All she needed to do was get out of her current relationship. In this mindset, she had exaggerated her groundless suspicions that Geoff was being unfaithful, or at least that he valued his job over his family. So she left. And this had redirected Geoff's unforgiveness away from his blood relatives towards her.

It surprised me – though I really don't know why, because I had been guilty of the same sin – that Geoff had been able to compartmentalise his personal and professional lives to such a degree.

Within this whole messy situation, which had developed over a period of many years, there were innumerable veins of corrosion which demons could occupy. The process was so insidious that no-one had noticed it; it would not be easy to unravel. Yet we were equally sure that it could be unravelled as all parties appeared to possess the basics of human decency. And Penny and I instinctively shared an almost perverse determination that Satan's wiles shouldn't prevail. Although there was no-one really to blame, it seemed clear to us that the point of attack would need to be Geoff's unforgiveness.

This wouldn't be easy. We were certain it would be inappropriate for Penny to go deep, one-to-one, with him. But if it was me, then I would blunder in without even the most rudimentary experience of counselling.

Yet it had to be me. So, I invited myself round the next weekend. When we met, we found ourselves able to dispense with preliminaries and went, without any diplomatic niceties, straight to the heart of the matter. I'd mentally rehearsed the more sensitive aspects of our talk on the assumption that Geoff might feel he was being judged or criticised if I didn't proceed with the lightest of touches. But none of this mattered. He recognised immediately the condition I described. He saw exactly what was causing the problem – it came as no surprise, though he had previously been unwilling to admit it in himself.

It didn't make Elisabeth's action any more morally justifiable, it didn't make his own behaviour any more defensible, it didn't make others' conduct any more forgivable. It just meant we all had our human frailties. This didn't mean we could justify ourselves or refuse to change, nor did it mean that others were obliged to accept us as we are. Neither, though, did it require us to become faultless saints overnight.

Geoff accepted that it meant a mixture of acceptance, change, vulnerability, pride, accommodation and all the other things that go with togetherness. This might sound impressive, and indeed it impressed me. But to be honest it evolved spontaneously as we talked for over an hour. Almost all of the questions and answers that I'd pre-rehearsed ahead of our meeting turned out to be superfluous.

And then, quite out of the blue, Geoff asked me to pray for him. Can you imagine it? A non-church-goer with a glacially rational mind, who opposes me steely-faced in business meetings, asking me to pray? But they do say that prayer is a universal, so perhaps I shouldn't have been so astonished.

I feigned ease. Of course, this was all strictly off the record. Monday morning would bring an alto-gether different set of behavioural norms.

So I smiled, said 'fine', and suggested an upturned-palm posture of prayer. I didn't even instruct him to close his eyes. I started with the words "... But I say unto you, love your enemies, bless them that curse you, do good to them that hate you, and pray for them who despitefully use you, and persecute you". I also included "Honour your father and mother". I was utterly astounded by Geoff's openness and will-ingness to confess his problem of unforgiveness. He was making himself vulnerable. Naturally, come Monday morning, normal business hostilities would be resumed. Even so, there was no going back in spiritual terms.

I left, saying that Penny and I would support him in prayer, and advising him not to expect a sudden breakthrough. I warned him that God's timing isn't the same as our timing, and – whilst I'm aware that non-Christians think this is just an escape clause for unanswered prayer – he seemed to accept it.

And we have been true to our word. He visits us weekly for a time of prayer although he's not yet ready to embrace the faith. I doubt if he fully understands why he's praying and we don't know how prayer is meant to work in such circumstances, but our times together are very real to him and he is visibly becoming a new person.

We don't really know what the current situation is with his family – why should we be the first to know? But there is a previously absent glint of happiness about his demeanour. Penny, whose radar is far more sensitive than mine about such matters, also thinks that things are changing for the better. One thing does seem clear to me, though: he has tuned into different timescales and to different understandings of mercy and forgiveness. I think he might even appreciate an invitation to join us at a morning service.

One day soon I'll pluck up the courage to ask him directly.

11. KAREN:

The Cross And
The Workplace

There are some people whom we are called to love rather than like. Loving, as unconditionally as humanly possible, is a general principle of Christian fellowship, but we cannot expect everybody to be to our taste. To be honest, Karen was not someone that Penny or I found it easy to get on with, and I strongly suspect we were not alone. There were few people more committed to humankind, more zealous in their faith or more generous of their time than Karen. Over the past twenty years, ever since she graduated from St Finnan's Youth Fellowship, she had been the workhorse of numerous sub-committees, working groups and rotas.

Despite her enthusiasm and gregariousness, Karen remained pigeonholed in our minds as one of the 'awkward brigade', a perception which was gently reinforced by many well-intentioned and non-judge-mental whispers that we heard from our fellow worshippers. I'm sure that several of her numerous acquaintances must have counted her as a genuine friend. She never appeared to be lonely, though we weren't surprised to learn that she had never married nor, by all accounts, ever been in so much as a medium-term relationship.

For all this, it still came as a shock to see her in the newspaper. Not so much surprised by her appearance – because she was often being quoted in the local weekly – but by the context in which she appeared. This time it was in a national tabloid and the headline read *Christian Worker Faces Dismissal For Wearing Cross*. Underneath was a photo of Karen, unmistakable with her Patagonian fleece and spinsterly bob of hair. Her face bore a characteristically determined grin, and below her chin was a choker chain with a simple cross, not quite large enough to be indiscreet.

I showed the article to Penny and, whilst she was obviously surprised, we exchanged knowing glances that conveyed a sense of inevitability. It was not the first time that such an incident had occurred, and I suppose many of us were becoming concerned that creeping forces of secularism were denying Christians rights which were assiduously afforded to other religions.

We could have predicted the contents of the article:

"Karen Fraser, 38, of Kilfinan has received a final warning from her employer, Smartprint, for refusing to remove an item of Christian jewellery. Karen has ignored warnings about jewellery not being permitted whilst operating machinery and instructions about not wearing it in the office. Ms Fraser told our reporter that she doesn't operate any hazardous machinery and that the item in question was close fitting and couldn't pose a risk to health and safety. It's something she'd always worn as an expression of her faith and the previous manager had never raised it as an issue. She felt it was a clear case of victimisation on religious grounds. A company spokeswoman declined to add to an earlier statement supporting the manager's stance and confirmed that Smartprint's health and safety policy was now being correctly enforced."

At first, I was a little put out that we had had to learn about this from the paper. I would have thought that Karen might have mentioned it to us beforehand. She wasn't usually reticent in bringing issues to our attention. The article suggested that the dispute had been rumbling on for a while, and that persuasion – hardly surprisingly – had failed.

Then I realised that, if Karen had sought my advice on it, I wouldn't have had a clue what to say. Looking down from my senior management perch, I suppose I would have meekly capitulated and accepted that rules were rules. But you could hardly say that to Karen.

I didn't have to wait long, however. That evening, Karen arrived at the door looking upbeat and determined. "You're a man who understands the world of work, aren't you Sam … ?"

Penny joined us, partly out of a genuine interest and desire to help, and partly for the entertainment value. Of course, hearing it from Karen's lips, the whole issue was black and white. Her line manager, Tricia, didn't like her because she felt threatened by Karen's experience and irreplaceability; Tricia just wanted a reason to cause trouble because she was a shallow materialist who thought all religious people were stupid. And the branch manager was a stickler for corporate policy who always took the line of least resistance.

Karen agreed that company policy banned jewellery in the interests of health and safety amongst staff who worked machinery. But, she insisted, no reasonable person could think that this really applied to a modest necklace when operating a photocopier and laminator. Her line manager had picked an argument with her purely to be vexatious and the branch manager had latched onto a legalistic interpretation of company policy that gave no latitude for individualism.

Up to this point we had listened to Karen's account attentively. It was, of course, vehement, partisan and internally consistent. Finally she said that if a Sikh or a Muslim had worn something indicative of their faith, the management would have bent over backwards in the interests of corporate inclusivity policy. The company was being vexatiously anti-Christian and she was determined to fight them, even if it meant being a martyr and appearing foolish in the eyes of the world. At this point, we couldn't help tacitly agreeing with her, even if we thought she was quite potty.

We talked around the options and whether there might be an alternative way. We didn't want her to lose her job. She wasn't especially well qualified and probably not as irreplaceable as she imagined, especially in the midst of a recession. These were things that we both intuitively agreed though would have couched only in the most diplomatic terms. We pussyfooted around the issue and suggested that there was little we could do, and were grateful that such situations hadn't arisen in our own workplaces. We knew that the weight of bureaucracy and legislation was against her, and that the media would enjoy the sport of throwing a Christian to the lions.

Of course, we parted friends, not least because we had provided Karen with a lively debate. She knew in her own heart that this was a straight fight between her and her employer, and that all she needed from us were some encouraging noises and a bit of mental sparring.

Thus it was that, a couple of weeks later, we read in the paper that an industrial tribunal was beckoning because neither side had been willing to compromise.

Much as we had reservations about Karen's stance, we did have a soft spot for her, and the following Sunday I included her in our prayers, naturally without dictating to the Lord which side He should take. She thanked me after the service and I suggested that she have one last go at speaking to someone further up the hierarchy. I knew the company's regional manager fairly well via the Rotary and suggested he might be receptive to a meeting. Perhaps they could find some accommodation and avoid a confrontation whose most likely outcome would inflict more damage on herself than the company. Martyrdom was rarely the optimum solution.

When she did speak to the regional manager the response was one which neither of us had expected.

The manager listened to her patiently, indeed at quite exceptional length, then took advantage of a pause in the tirade to politely suggest a meeting with none other than the company CEO. This offer momentarily silenced Karen. It was almost like Paul appealing to Caesar. How could she refuse?

And so, at the eleventh hour as we might say, she travelled to Edinburgh to meet a steely-faced, impeccably besuited CEO. Some people exude authoritative dynamism and Malcolm Weekes was one of them. Karen would have worn her solitary posh frock if she'd given the matter forethought and was uncharacteristically abashed by her casual appearance, but Weekes hardly seemed to notice. She had viewed the gender-stereotypical image of the traditional patrician with disdain, but she now rapidly revised her opinion. Weekes exuded a charisma far beyond that of the usual "suit".

He invited her to set out her case and listened with intent, though to her credit Karen was unusually succinct and reasonable. He flexed his fingers, then rested his chin on them.

"Now Ms Fraser – might I call you Karen?" he started. She nodded.

"Well, Karen, Smartprint may be a big company but we do value our employees. We especially appreciate loyalty. How long have you worked for us? Twenty years? Well, I'm sorry that it has come to this, because the last thing I want is for our staff to feel we don't care for them."

Karen bore an expression of cautious reassurance.

"But of course," Weekes continued, "we do have company rules that are there for a purpose. Indeed, I helped to write most of them. I'd like to reassure you that we'd enforce rules regardless – we are no respecter of persons."

Weekes's use of a biblical phrase was sufficient to wrong-foot Karen, and stayed her impulse to inter-ject.

He stared pensively at her, as if trying to think of a mutually agreeable solution.

"Tell me, Karen", he said at length. "What are you wearing?"

It was a most peculiar question, but the faint smile on his face made Karen feel she could commence her reply with a nervous laugh.

"Slacks, sweatshirt..", she started.

"And...?"

"And a necklace. With a cross on it."

"And...?

Her mind went blank. Surely he wasn't wanting her to discuss her shoes. A horrible thought struck her. Perhaps he was a pervert, mentally undressing her? But suddenly her thoughts were floored by a most unanticipated comment.

"What about a breastplate of righteousness?"

She was silenced. Such utter loss for words was beyond her previous experience. She could do nothing other than wait for his next observation.

"Or the belt of truth? Or the helmet of salvation? I can see you wearing them."

Karen's eyes started to water with shock. So the CEO was a Christian? Surely he couldn't therefore object to her wearing a cross?

"You see, I've thought and prayed about this a lot," said Weekes, as straight as a die. "What I would really like is if you gracefully agreed to stop wearing adornments whilst at work, but let people see your faith in other ways."

This wasn't a suggestion Karen had anticipated. Even so, she suddenly found her voice and her unerring instinct to disagree.

"But I don't want to just keep my faith to myself. I want to proclaim it visibly. I want people to see a cross every time they come into my office."

Weekes thought carefully. "Just because they don't see a symbol," he said, "doesn't mean to say they don't see Christ."

Again, she was floored. She could hardly believe the words that this hard-bitten self-made millionaire was saying. Yet she wasn't fazed. The unanticipated turn of events had given her renewed boldness. Eschewing her sense of diplomacy, minimal at the best of times, she replied, "But if you keep your religion to yourself how are people going to become aware of Christ?"

There was a brief silence, in which Karen seized the opportunity to confront Weekes more directly: "Do people here even know that you're a Christian?"

Her tone was so accusatory that it would normally have caused significant offence, especially to a person of authority. But Weekes remained placid, even affectionate. "Oh yes they do. Oh yes they do," was all he said, but he said it in such a way that she was in no doubt about its veracity.

And as Karen thought about it, she realised that the whole atmosphere of the headquarters, daunting though the buildings and corridors may have been, was one of humanity and value.

"I'd still like to wear my cross just so that everyone can see it when they walk in."

By now, she expected a concession and was surprised when she didn't get one. "In that case," said Weekes, "I would have to back my colleagues. But think about this. You're quite unlikely to win converts amongst people who casually walk into your office and who may or may not notice that you are wearing a particular piece of jewellery. It's much more likely that you'll win over individuals whom you work alongside on a day to day basis and who gradually come to discover your values and beliefs. Can't you wear those instead?"

Karen thought very carefully indeed. "If I capitulate, the press will have a field day saying I've been defeated. Atheists one, Christians nil."

Weekes held up his hand.

"If you graciously agree to adhere to company policy, I'll make sure that your faith gets very good media coverage," he insisted

Karen looked sceptical, even confrontational, so Weekes quickly added, "Oh yes I will! Oh yes I will!"

Nowadays, Karen – reluctantly it must be said – doesn't wear jewellery during the working day, though outside working hours she sports a rather fetching silver cross which Penny and I gave her as a birthday present. What she has noticed, however, is that more than one colleague has asked her about her faith whilst no-one was looking.

Indeed, two employees of Smartprint have recently started attending St Finnan's. I won't insult your intelligence by telling you the reason.

12. ELLIE:

First Impressions

First impressions always count in business, perhaps more than they should, but it's an inviolable law. By that standard, Penny and I would quickly have dismissed Ellie as a lonely widow, with no way of filling the hole in her life other than to immerse herself in the minutiae of church protocols.

St Finnan's Lay Reader was silver-haired, rather prim, almost militaristically upright, and neither short nor tall. She held conversation comfortably, without being needlessly talkative. She seemed to have few opinions despite an evident level of education. Perhaps she was late sixties, though possessed with a nervous energy and in no imminent risk of dotage. In sum, she gave the firm impression of being a reliable, unimaginative workhorse dutifully pottering away in the background, on whom the clergy had depended rather longer and more extensively than was desirable.

We had initially gleaned a little about her from Max, though we hadn't enquired with any great curiosity and he had proffered only sparse insight.

We learned she had had a lifelong attachment to St Finnan's, and trained to be a lay reader in her forties, whilst still working for some company or other. After her husband died prematurely, she benefited from a significant life assurance policy. Very soon afterwards, the opportunity of early retirement arose, subsequent to which she filled the gaps in church roles that weren't already filled by others. In sum, she fitted our identikit perfectly. Every church should have a widow or spinster like Ellie, and generally does.

We had invited her round to supper one evening some weeks after we arrived, to discuss her concerns about the amount of pressure that Max was under. This fellowship allowed us to detect that there was perhaps rather more to her than initially met the eye. She bore none of the awkwardness that we had anticipated. She was a curiously accomplished blend of privacy and candour, self-effacement and social ease. We couldn't gauge how intelligent she was but then I've increasingly learned that such judgements are very subjective. Certainly she had abundant common sense, and could go straight to the nub of an issue with a sharp eye for pertinent and unadorned detail.

We had initially concluded that Max over-depended on her out of necessity. He desperately needed someone to fill gaps in rotas, prepare information for meetings and sacrifice their evenings. In turn, she probably needed something to fill her time and give her a feeling of self-worth.

But from that first occasion when we shared fellowship together we began to suspect that there was something more to her than met the eye. She was actually jolly competent and well-integrated, and could doubtless have found a dozen other ways of keeping herself occupied. She was a mainstay of St Finnan's because she enjoyed it rather than because she craved acceptance.

That evening, we had invited her with a clear purpose in mind – to discuss ways of alleviating the unhealthy levels of pressure on Max. But she was blessed with sufficient airs and graces not to lunge abruptly into business matters. She was concerned about Max – that was clear – but not so blinkered that she forgot to ask about how we were settling into St Finnan's and whether we were missing our previous existence. She asked about our family and work in ways that showed genuine interest and insight. It was little surprise that everyone spoke well of her, even those who had opposed women servers and, in turn, women priests. And yet she hovered inconspicuously out of the limelight, more than content to remain a lay reader whilst doubtless having had the potential to have been an excellent priest if she had so aspired.

And when she did broach her plot about allowing Max to take a break, she was so well organised and matter-of-fact that we couldn't help but agree. In fact, she practically made us feel as if it had been our idea in the first place.

Of course, she didn't want to spend the whole evening talking about church business. She knew precisely when the topic had been sufficiently aired. Then she deflected the conversation to social matters, and succeeded in finding out more about us than we about her.

Indeed, we found out little more than we already knew, apart from the fact that she didn't have any children, for whatever reason, but which didn't seem to have left any emotional lacunae. She gave the quiet impression of someone who was content to have had led a full life, and continued to lead one.

I got to know her rather better during Max's unofficial sabbatical, during which we worked together closely and often. Her inadvertent asides betrayed an acute knowledge of literature, classical music, history and, rather more surprisingly, science. I was no longer surprised that she was skilled in extracting information from me about the past and able to show an intelligent awareness in my particular field of structural engineering. Perhaps there was the mildest hint of envy towards my new role in senior management, or maybe it was just curiosity. Ellie seemed content with what she had accomplished – and what she was continuing to achieve – rather than embittered at missed opportunities.

It was left to Penny to unravel a little more of her past, midway through our first year. Having first pigeonholed her as an historically redundant female role model, willingly sidelined to backroom drudgery, Penny had latterly reckoned her as decidedly inspirational. Whilst Penny had initially expected to enlighten Ellie, it turned out to be the other way round.

They were in the vestry together preparing for a communion service when Ellie asked her how the preparations for ordination training were going. Ordination was still very much 'Plan A' at that time, its onset having merely been deferred by our change in circumstances. But Penny was unexpectedly to learn a little more about herself and her aspirations.

"Do you think that priesthood's always the right calling?", Ellie had asked her.

"No, not for everyone. But I'm certain I want to commit to ministry full-time, rather than serve in the wings, like Sam. That's fine for him, because he's always been an engineer at heart and always will be. I want to be involved in the church first and foremost. I want to be a change-maker. The church has to transform itself into something that's going to work in the third millennium. I want to be part of that change."

It was a well thought through statement of fact, honed over many years, and one which she hadn't expected to be challenged.

"It's just that I've been wondering whether God wants you to be a change-maker in that way. There are different ways in which we serve. I think you have a gift for counselling. People like your practicality more than your theory."

Penny had bristled, but without protest. She could sense Ellie pausing whilst gauging whether it was safe to continue. Shortly, she did. "I've heard people talk about your particular type of wisdom. About things like work-life balance and working one's way through life's difficulties. You know, I've come to realise that the Kingdom of God is advanced one person at a time, through wise counsel, rather than hundreds at a time by erudite preaching. Or at least, that's how it usually happens. Please think about it."

There was no opportunity to contradict Ellie's proposition, because it was time to swing into action as the service started. But, despite Penny's later protestations that she wasn't really a people person and that she was much more the strategic organisational thinker, Ellie kept insisting that her no-nonsense and worldly-wise approach was precisely what suited her to an alternative ministry. Something to do with being alongside people in their everyday situations rather than being a career-track clergywoman. And her experience in the world of business enabled her to reach parts of people's daily lives that she and Max couldn't, given the pressure of church commitments.

Penny struggled with Ellie's comments that evening, perhaps even to the point of resentment. And despite my saccharine reassurances that of course the priesthood had always been and always would be her calling, I kept being nagged by the thought that perhaps Ellie was right. In fact, by now my over-riding impression of Ellie was that she was invariably right, perhaps because she was so cautious in venturing an opinion in the first place. Indeed, I too had been similarly affronted by Ellie's home truths in the past, when she would casually and disarmingly observe where my own strengths and weaknesses might lie.

Thereafter, Penny and Ellie had many heart-to-hearts, and I was only privy to a small sample of what they discussed. But we learned that Ellie had had a successful career in microbiology, which had never progressed to the levels it might have done, due to her unstinting involvement in St Finnan's. She had good reason to be bitter – a very close marriage which had been prematurely curtailed and two miscarriages – but she never bore any resentment because she believed that God had a better plan. Rarely had we met such contentment and rarely had we encountered such prayerful wisdom.

Ellie has made us think again, both about the hands we have been dealt in the past and about our intentions for the future. But we have also been challenged by the way we pigeonhole and label people. In our competitive world of trade and commerce we always tend to judge according to first impressions, and we wear masks that present an unreal face to the world. But we were reminded that God doesn't see things the way that we see them; we judge by outward appearance, but God looks at the heart.

Gradually, falteringly, we have begun to see what God sees in Ellie. She is that rare creature who has discerned and followed her unglamorous but profoundly effective vocation. She has learned to be content in every situation. There is a great deal of Mary in her: she flourishes through her obedience to God and in consequence brings out the best in others.

We had judged by outward appearances. Ellie, without an ounce of judgement, had carefully peeled away our masks and pierced through to those lingering pockets of self which we hadn't yet surrendered. She saw not as we saw; she looked on the inner person.

13. PIRAN:

An Embarrassment of Parents

I guess you won't have heard about Bridget and me yet? That would be typical of Mum and Dad. They just tend to refer to 'the kids' and forget we've got names.

Not names that either of us are terribly keen on, to be honest, though they've proved a conversation piece over the years. Mum and Dad discovered Celtic Christianity when they were at university and we subsequently suffered from obscure saints names. At least, as they often reminded us, "they are names that are difficult to shorten".

From what I can work out – though Mum and Dad never actually said, but it isn't rocket science to do the sums – they got married within a few months of graduating, not least because I was already an embryo at that stage.

Anyway, Bridget and I have a little conspiracy. To our amazement, Mum and Dad have made it to their silver wedding. Before they moved from Lincolnshire it seemed an unlikely prospect, but you never know what to expect with parents. So here we are in Kilfinan to give them an anniversary surprise. They told us they weren't planning anything special. Perhaps just a dinner at a decent restaurant or a weekend away.

But we can't let them off as easily as that. Given the size of our student loans – I'm halfway through my Masters and Bridget's in the final year of her Psychology degree – we can't afford a big present. But Mum's brothers and Dad's sister are fortunately quite well off and have clubbed together to buy them a cruise from Greenock, so we're up here to do the presentation and set up a Skype link with our aunt and uncles.

We had been exercising our minds as to how to avoid arousing suspicion. We've each only been to see the new house once, so Mum in particular would have smelt a rat if we'd actually got round to coordinating a joint visit.

And then Dad provided us with the perfect cover. As chance would have it, his company were having a pre-Christmas works 'do', to which we were cordially invited. Groan! He assured us that it was a family event and there would be people of our own age, but I'd heard him say this before about works and church events which turned out to be unimaginably excruciating. What's the collective noun for parents: an 'embarrassment' perhaps? To be honest, the whole thing sounded dismal, but the timing was perfect – just a couple of days before their anniversary.

We aren't a particularly close family; nothing dysfunctional or hostile, but just not particularly close, either emotionally or geographically. Bridget's quite like Mum in lots of ways and they quickly home in on the same wavelength whenever they're together. But equally she's always been something of a Daddy's girl and she took it really hard when their marriage was going through a bad patch; she empathised with both sides equally and it tore her apart. She just kept saying to me that she hoped it would all blow over which, in the end, it did. I'm more like Dad, the nerdy engineer, so emotional intelligence has never really been my strong point.

But, even so, my empathic skills have had to ascend an almost vertical learning curve lately, because Bridget's long-term relationship has just broken down and she's been turning to me every evening for long-distance consolation via text and email. Really rotten thing to happen just before Christmas, especially with finals round the corner. I was hoping this escapade up north might at least provide her with a distraction.

Anyway, it was brilliant to see her again at Glasgow airport. We lead very different lives these days and meet up much less often than we should. When you permanently rely on virtual contact, you forget what it's actually like being with someone in person. We took the short cut to Kilfinan via the ferry and Mum and Dad met us at the pier head. They looked really happy and at ease. Life in these latitudes must be doing them good.

Then there's the house. Bridget and I agreed we both wanted a house like this. Loads of space, glorious peace, breathtaking views, snow on the hills. We even found it difficult to believe the tales of wintry gloom, because when we arrived there was a crystal clear low-angle sunlight that gave a Renaissance geometry to the whole landscape. We seemed a million miles from our rabbit hutch university residences.

Of course, you've got to put up with the religious paraphernalia around the house. But actually Mum and Dad aren't too bad. We'd been round to some of their friends who were really weird with Bible verses and icons on the walls, but Mum and Dad are relatively discreet, I think because they weren't from religious families and our late grandparents had found their student conversions a bit strange. We had to do the church thing as children, of course, but fortunately Mum and Dad didn't force it down our throats or they'd have put us off for life. As it was, they were placated by the fact that we'd at least described ourselves as Christian in the Census, and were willing to give St Finnan's a try whilst we were up.

As you might expect, once we were inside the house, Mum was all over Bridget because of her break-up, which wasn't entirely appreciated because sis was trying hard to give the impression of being totally over it.

Dad suggested it would be a good idea for us to leave the girls together for a chat. So we headed into the hills behind the house for a walk. Not a serious climb, more of a forest trail with some beauty spots, but it took us over an hour and we had plenty of opportunity to talk. He was very interested in my progress as a Civil Engineer, of course, because I suspect he's deeply envious of me doing a Master's at Imperial. He sang the praises of engineers like Watt and Telford and suggested we take a trip to the West Highlands some time to study the viaducts and canals. He's actually pretty smart, and only stage-manages the impression of being a plodder in order to wrong-foot the opposition. I learned this at quite an early age.

Of course he asked me all the usual father-son stuff about what I was planning to do in life and whether I'd got a steady girlfriend, which I side-stepped because the answers were "don't know" and "not yet" respectively. I was also being super-evasive because sis and I had to be careful not to spill the beans about the anniversary surprise. Anyway it was a great walk and I was too distracted by the scenery to talk about anything particularly deep.

Mum always amazes me when she does the house-wife bit, and she couldn't have been more of a fifties role model when she produced a traditional high tea on our return. She'd even got Bridget to bake some delicious drop scones and I have to say, in the least patronising way possible of course, that one of these days sis will make someone a great wife. "You'll need something to tide you over till the evening," Mum assured us. I'm not sure whether she genuinely enjoys the domestic stuff or whether, deep down and despite the businesslike exterior, she's actually quite vulnerable and craves acceptance. That's one mystery I think I'll never manage to fathom.

Rather too soon, Dad began to get fidgety as to whether we had suitable clothes for the works 'do'. Actually, we surprised them by how well we scrubbed up. I'd just bought myself an interview suit which Mum said made me look really fanciable whilst Bridget, after she'd finally emerged from an hour in the *ensuite*, looked distinctly gorgeous in a classy little tea dress. Even I noticed it had a delicate *art nouveau* print, and I can't remember when I last gave a totally spontaneously comment to a girl on how lovely she looked.

However, that was the easy bit. In truth, Bridget and I were both terrified about what this works 'do' might involve. We had been told it was a type of dance-plus-supper; a *ceilidh*. I'd once seen an advert for one in the Student Union, and had joked about it, disparagingly. Clubbing was one thing; a traditional dance with lots of bagpipes and accordions, and oldsters talking about work was something quite different. We anticipated a long evening with other bored offspring at the bar, awkwardly fishing around for topics of conversation. A long and cringeworthy night beckoned.

We arrived at the Marine Hotel at 7.30. There was a curiously pervasive air of decayed grandeur about the place. I could imagine the shipmasters and landed gentry staying here a hundred years ago, feasting on venison and grouse. It looked as if nowadays it mainly depended on coach parties and tribute nights, though there was a modern gym offering temporary membership which looked worth a visit if I came up again.

Dad led us through the lounge bar to a suite with a ballroom which opened out onto the most fantastic view of the sea. The place was already getting busy and the age range must have been from five to six-ty-five. Thankfully, there was a healthy sprinkling of teens and twenties and Dad introduced us to another family who had three sons either side of twenty, who enthusiastically welcomed us. But the most striking thing was that they were wearing kilts – "Highland Dress" as Mum diplomatically reminded me. I'd only seen it in photographs before and thought it was a tourist gimmick, but seeing them so confident in their culture actually made me quite envious. And Bridget's eyes were on stalks.

Euan, the eldest one, and closest in age to me, offered me a pint of the local brew, which seemed a bit fizzy and fresh at first, but to which I adjusted very quickly.

"He's a bit religious, your Dad, isn't he?" Euan said in a way that was obviously intended as a non-threat-ening ice-breaker.

"Yes, we've learned to live with that. I think he's mostly harmless."

"Oh, I don't think it does him any harm. He's the sort who can get away with talking about church stuff. He's very popular, you know. Well, according to my Dad, he is. And is that your Mum?" He nodded in her direction.

"Yes, that's her. The *Pennyweight*," I grinned. "Networking as usual."

And as I looked across at them I noticed how relaxed they appeared. Slotting in amongst friends; at ease with themselves and with their company. I'm sure that was the first time I'd ever looked at my parents and almost envied them.

"Look out," yelled one of the girls at the bar. "Here comes Cammie and the band."

'Cammie' was what I would have described as a 'caller'. I'd been to some barn dances in the past where you have someone who calls out the steps whilst the band plays some corny dance tunes and everyone's got to join in and shout 'yee-hah'. It brought back hideous memories. Then a group of rather ageing musicians trooped in after him – fiddle, accordion, guitar and something like a big round hand-held drum. Surely not three hours of this?

The youths around us looked inexplicably excited. My worst suspicions were aroused. I had finally reached the Ultima Thule of Hicksville. If this was the high spot, what were the low spots like?

Apparently, we were to start with something called a Strathspey, and a couple of dozen older couples moved into the dancing area. Embarrassingly, they included Mum and Dad, who had joined in after some heckling. Well, at least they certainly seemed popular. Then the music started and it struck me as something like a waltz. I had done ballroom at school, and am reasonably accomplished and innately well balanced, so I pick up dance steps pretty well. Not as well as sis, though – she's a natural gymnast and adores anything to do with dance.

I found it all rather sad – not only because Mum and Dad looked like doe-eyed teenagers on their first date, but also because I felt like I'd been dragged back into pre-history. Bridget's face was a picture too; a study in mortified disbelief. What made it even sadder was that the local youth seemed to be taking it all so seriously. They were actually appreciating the dances and lapping up the bumpkin music. I wished the ground would swallow me up.

Then something even worse happened. When the dance ended, Cammie turned in our direction and said:

"Now come on youngsters, don't prop up the bar all night. Yes, even you Stephen. Take your hand off that pint and put it round the lassie next to you."

Stephen turned bright red and hesitantly complied. This was truly humiliating.

"We're going to dance a reel called *Miss Johnstone of Ardrossan*", continued the caller.

There was an inexplicable cheer from the assembled gathering.

And then the youngsters around me started to move towards the dance floor. I began to panic. Oh, please no! It looked like one of those appalling country dances that I'd had to do at primary school when you kept having to swing around with a succession of sweaty palmed giggling girls.

Bridget was suddenly whisked away, after a very cursory but disarmingly gracious invitation from Euan. I froze to the spot, unable to retreat but equally unwilling to advance. My decision was made for me when a lithe and confident blonde girl, who introduced herself as Fiona, dragged me towards the circle saying, "Come on, Piran, don't be shy."

I protested that I hadn't a clue what to do, but she assured me she'd teach me the steps in no time. Actually, I did find them quite straightforward, and clearly impressed her with my natural facility. By the time we progressed to our next partner I was well into the swing of things and by the time I progressed to Fiona once more we were able to converse about each other rather than about dance steps. It transpired she was a final year medical student at Aberdeen and I was rather chuffed at having my first ever dance with a future doctor.

The dance was distinctly energetic and we all looked a little flushed by the end. The band took a couple of minutes to re-group its resources, which gave me time to get a round in, not least because I was keen to buy a drink for Euan, to whom Bridget was now clinging like a limpet. But we didn't have a lot of time for recovery because we were rudely cajoled into something called the Highland Rambler which had a rather tricky way of casting off, and I had to listen to Fiona's instructions extremely carefully. However, I negotiated it without serious disaster, after which we were given a decent spell for recuperation.

It transpired that the lads were great rugby aficionados and, indeed, I could see how Euan would make an excellent lock forward. However, I trumped him by saying that Imperial College Rugby Soc had got tickets for the Calcutta Cup at Twickenham. He turned visibly green on the spot, but took it with good humour. If Bridget were to get caught on the rebound, I wouldn't mind it being to a chap like Euan.

A couple of dances later and the caller announced that food would shortly be ready. Glancing at my watch I was surprised to discover it was after half eight; contrary to my fears, time had flown by.

However, there was to be some sort of medley inflicted on us first. There was a good natured groan from the audience as the caller attempted to explain a complex sequence of steps, and this time I really did have to concentrate on Fiona's explanation of a petronella, though it seemed logical enough once you'd got the hang of it. This time the dance floor was overwhelmingly dominated by the younger set, the energy and confidence of anyone over forty having been temporarily sapped.

Anyway, we were ultimately allowed to depart for the function suite where Dad's firm had laid on the most fantastic spread. I was about to head straight for the chicken wings when I felt Euan place his hand on my right shoulder and realised the kilties were all staring at me. With a rugby player's vice-like grip he marched me to a plate of haggis balls and required me to undergo a forfeit. I was to eat at least three of them. I eyed the grotesque bush tucker with terror but, unable to decline with dignity, accepted the challenge and eventually admitted to finding them rather palatable.

My challenge having been discharged with honour, we compared notes about the evening and our parents' work associates. I was surprised to learn that Bridget had been spontaneously re-christened Bridie, a name which is apparently affectionately associated with a saint around these parts. Anyway, she seemed perfectly content with the abbreviation. It was great to see her looking happy after all she'd gone through of late.

What really struck me though was the way that Dad looked so relaxed amongst his colleagues. I'd never noticed before how easily he could converse with everyone from the MD to the receptionist. Mum came over to check how we were all doing and was quickly on first name terms with all the girls, before rejoining an influential looking coterie of power dressers.

When we'd been out walking, Dad had said something about all the workplace being a mission field. At the time, this worried me, because I'd visualised him trying to buttonhole people in the corridor and convert them, but he'd assured me it was nothing like that. Now I could begin to see what he meant. He was clearly genuinely interested in these people, even though they weren't overtly religious. He sustained their confidence. They held him in affection. You could see it quite clearly.

I'd never seen him in that light before. When we were in Lincolnshire, Mum and Dad were always surrounded by loads of churchy people. Now they were just being normal, among a lot of other regular workmates. I could see what he meant about colleagues valuing someone whom they could talk to about spiritual matters. I could understand what he meant when he spoke about a 'calling'. I even began to wish that I'd had the occasional opportunity to talk to a spiritual confidant who wasn't actually wearing a dog collar.

Seeing him in that way made me think quite seriously about coming back to church, even though I really had difficulty with the resurrection and miracles and all that sort of stuff. I wondered how many of his colleagues thought the same.

Anyway, before I knew it, it was time for another round of dancing. Mum and Dad were back sitting next to each other, and it was weird seeing them like that. Actually, I felt quite smug. It's not every day that you can view your parents in a sentimental light; vulnerably naïve; smooching like teenagers; totally unsuspecting their anniversary surprise. It struck me that the tables had been well and truly turned. For once, Bridget and I held the trump card over this starry-eyed couple.

And my strange feeling of control was reinforced when I smiled across to Bridget – or perhaps I should now call her Bridie, which sounds so much nicer. I'd never seen her look so amusingly doe-eyed. Ah well; she couldn't ask for better company than Euan on a night like this.

It was all good spectator sport, as I prepared to get another round of drinks in and talk rugby with the lads. But I was interrupted by the caller announcing that we'd be doing another slow Strathspey. Slightly different this time – non-progressive, so we'd keep the same partner throughout. The boys definitely agreed this was one for the parents. I prepared to sit it out and planted myself firmly on a bar stool.

But then I noticed Fiona's piercing blue eyes staring in my direction. Well, it would be bad manners to refuse…

14. PENNY:
Home Truths

You've heard enough from Sam, so let me tell this my way. Don't take everything he tells you at face value anyway. He's as honest as the day's long but sometimes he has a rather creative view of reality.

I'll admit I was in a bad place spiritually and emotionally before we moved to Kilfinan. I was ready to walk out on Sam, go it alone. Although we didn't realise it at first, we'd been growing apart for years. Nothing dramatic. We'd practised a polite civility. Merely two very different personalities with different interests, moving in our separate directions. It took a university reunion to wake me up to what was happening. An old friend from the Christian Union confided in me that Sam and I had always been seen as the odd couple – me the ambitious buzzy type and Sam the unadventurous plodder. A quarter of a century barely seemed to have taken any toll on her, and I felt distinctly jaded and saggy in her presence. Perhaps a new start was just what I needed.

The children were the main thing that kept us together, but very soon we'd be empty nesters.

Indeed, our offspring had become remarkably independent and self-reliant even during their final years at school. People at church would have been surprised if we'd separated – they saw us as the perfect Christian couple – but that image was increasingly a façade. Sam was, despite his businesslike exterior, really quite domesticated and he invariably took the line of least resistance.

There's no doubt that I would have found it easier to leave than he would; he'd probably have taken it hard, though there were occasions when I wondered if he'd even notice. Sam was part of the woodwork at St John's but I had comparatively few ties and would have readily found myself a new spiritual home.

Sam had toyed with full-time ministry for a long while, but I knew he'd never do it. Too many hard decisions. In the end, he opted for Reader training, something which didn't exactly thrill me because he already spent far too little time doing anything useful around the house. Yet I conceded that it was the right time for him. He was in control of his job, creating spaces in the day that hadn't previously been there. We weren't getting any younger and, unless we took our mid-life opportunities, the chances of being approved for training would quickly diminish. He had a ministry, it was clear. And he would be supporting our over-worked ministry team in our large suburban parish.

We'd agreed it was my turn next. My decision would be of a different magnitude, and I needed to give it more thought. I wouldn't be satisfied with a lay readership; I was confident my calling was to the priesthood, albeit juggled with the safety net of a freelance business sideline. Also, I'd reached a critical stage at work, trying to claw my way to a position of responsibility after career breaks, and I was determined to gain a decent promotion as a basis for setting up my own consultancy. I was impressing my colleagues with my command of marketing, just as I was impressing the diocese with my theological verve. In my imaginings I was amongst the first wave of Church of England female bishops, taking my diocese into exciting new areas of faith and outreach. I would be lauded for my achievements in connecting with the unchurched via my business-world savviness.

To his credit, the priest at St John's gave me ample opportunity to develop my goals. I pressed all the right buttons with the hierarchy; my preaching was considered elegant and effective and, ironically, my 'churchmanship' deemed modern and progressive without being divisive. Ministerial training quickly became an all-or-nothing approach for me. Yet I still had things to achieve at work and a pension pot to consolidate, so it seemed appropriate to defer my training until after Sam was licensed. There would still be time to seek ordination and the clergy quietly assured me there would be an accelerated career track awaiting me.

If that all sounds very neat and consensual, I'm afraid I'll have to disappoint. The strategy was, in hindsight, almost entirely of human construction. Looking back I realise how much I was trusting in my own strength. I'd never believed in the devil – I was far too modern for that. Surely, the notion of a (male) Tempter was just a medieval fiction to control the restive masses? Latterly, though, I've become receptive to the idea of a malevolent and deceptive power at work making us follow the way of self, kidding us that we're listening to God.

But I digress. Just after he'd been licensed as a reader, Sam announced that he was being moved up to some northern wilderness. It came like a bolt of the blue, and I'm ashamed to admit that I swore at him like a trooper. In my defence, I just didn't believe his version of the story. If he'd said that the company was devolving, and they'd offered him an attractive promotion opportunity at a northern depot that was being upgraded to a regional headquarters, then I might have cut him more slack. If he'd asked me whether it was a good idea for him to accept the offer, knowing that the alternative was falling off the company radar and being passed over for future promotion, I'd have given serious thought to the possibility.

But being presented with a *fait accompli*, a decision that he said was simply beyond his control and non-negotiable, raised my hackles. I felt he was covering up for personal ambition; I felt unspeakably betrayed. If, indeed, there was any truth in the matter, then it just showed the ease with which he was manipulated.

It was our most difficult time so far, and I was determined to give him as much grief as possible. I mentally perfected a theology of the honourable divorce, which I had convinced myself would win powerful allies in certain quarters of the church. At least I could revert to my maiden name and avoid the wearisome quips about being a *pennyweight*.

In the end something held me back from walking out on him. Looking back, I'm sure that that 'something' was God speaking to me, but at the time I rationalised it as not wanting to upset the kids when they were facing critical exams at university. Indeed, I prided myself on my – admittedly grudging – submission to authority.

Coincidentally – so I supposed – my employer had announced a voluntary redundancy scheme with a very narrow window, days after Sam was licensed. Recently promoted, I was in a good position to receive a handsome payoff which in turn could be used as seedcorn for setting up as a sole trader. Rationally, I could move to anywhere in the country that had decent broadband.

I spoke to the rural dean about my ministerial prospects and he reassured me about training opportunities in the Scottish Episcopal church with which – again entirely coincidentally – he had strong family connections. There was a twinkle in his eye when he suggested that the 'piskies' might be more fleet-footed than the Church of England in promoting women to senior positions.

Thus it was that, through gritted teeth, I decided to stand by Sam. I agreed we might as well visit the area, which we did one grey weekend in June. A quick scan of the house prices confirmed we could enjoy a much improved standard of living. The town centre, despite looking a bit depressed and dour, had a reasonable range of shops. I persuaded myself it was workable and, as Sam reminded me, Lincolnshire is hardly the cultural nexus of the universe. After that, things happened too quickly to brood upon. Sam's employer didn't waste time in relocating him and in a matter of weeks we were moving north.

We moved into our new house one day in late summer when it was raining stair-rods. I'd left most of the house-hunting to Sam because I couldn't be bothered with the repeated traipse up to Kilfinan, and I only had a hazy recall of our new home. It seemed grey and austere when we arrived and I took to bed that night exhausted, regretful and resentful. I was woken at five by sunlight streaming in through the blankets which served as our makeshift curtains. I hadn't realised that being a couple of degrees further north would make such a difference to daybreak. I dragged myself up past a gently snoring Sam to close the gap in the curtains.

Then I noticed a perfect summer dawn. Drawing the blanket aside I gazed across a serene, fjord-like sea loch. Beyond it were mountains cloaked in forest and heather moorland. The mauves and pinks of the sky, intensified by the northerly sun's angle of incidence, scattered across the water. I scanned the almost deserted coast road and saw houses and cottages spread out in generous gardens rather than hunched together in a suburban huddle. I decided I could live with this, after all.

We took the usual couple of weeks to settle in, all of which provided a useful distraction from the necessity of producing my business plan and applying for a start-up account. By the end of the month I was finding my way around the town and accustoming myself to the idiosyncrasies of our new church and its diocesan personnel, as well as bringing my ministerial aspirations to their attention. Having made the decision to see it through I must admit that I felt a very strong sense of inner peace. Following that first morning when I drew back the curtains, I was surprised to discover in the following weeks that I was happier than I'd been for years.

What took me much longer to get used to was the people and their way of life. There was a strikingly different character and tempo here, and I was sufficiently worldly wise not to offend our host population by speaking out of turn. It was obvious that we were viewed as outsiders, and would remain so for at least twenty years. The people were perceptibly friendlier if somewhat guarded, and I had to check my native bluntness on numerous occasions. Despite their outward hospitality, I constantly had the impression of treading on eggshells; yet, however frustrating I might have found their mores, I was determined to achieve 'local' status as soon as possible.

Not least, this was because I needed to gain people's trust. Of course, my game plan was still to train for the ministry as soon as the church would allow, and get my own parish. We had the sort of marriage that could work if we had to live apart most of the week, and might even work better. However, to begin with I needed a soft landing from my day job as well as an income of my own. The more materialistic corners of my soul craved a cushion against the penury of full time ministry, something which I scarcely rationalised at the time. So I had to set up my own business and accumulate a client list. I was at the mercy of the goodwill of the local populace, including the various worthies who were my passport to friendship and business networks.

My initial impressions of St Finnan's were mixed. There was much to like about the Reverend Max Maxwell and his little band of helpers; the building was delightful; the Celtic nuances of the music surprisingly pleasant; and there was a talented nucleus to the congregation. The ministry team were very encouraging and helpful to me in terms of my aspirations, and of course they would have quickly given Sam a full-time workload if he'd permitted them. But it was rather too small a church for my liking. And, at the end of the day, as a place to develop an influential ministry, it was a backwater.

We had managed to build our church in Lincolnshire up to a regular congregation of around two hundred, rising sharply at major festivals. When we moved there, it was struggling and had an unhealthy turnover of clergy, but stability was brought by a new vicar who was at least receptive if not exactly dynamic. It was also blessed with an energetic lay ministry team with which we progressively engaged ourselves.

But St Finnan's was a modest church with a regular congregation of 60-odd, rising on high days and holy days to a hundredish. It played third fiddle numerically to the Church of Scotland and Evangelical Free Church and was about on a par with the Catholics;

it was a bit bigger than a couple of other churches that didn't show up on my initial radar. It was also part of a surprisingly active inter-church group that undertook a range of good deeds. As ever, with an Episcopal church hereabouts, it was part of a shared benefice, within which a hard-pressed rector spread himself across two other tiny but idyllic churches in outlying villages.

After a while, though, I started to get into the rhythm of things. The sense of provincial isolation diminished and I became aware of facets to Kilfinan life that were really quite cosmopolitan. There was a distinctive cadence to the way of life and a character to the people. And, of course, the relative proximity to Glasgow gave me a bolthole whenever our little cocoon became too claustrophobic.

Nor was St Finnan's the slowly withering, introspective holy huddle I'd feared. Despite the absence of coloured skins and social diversity, there was somehow more of life's rich tapestry, need and wisdom than I'd experienced in previous churches. The congregation were an interesting and eclectic bunch. Once you gauged their cultural quirks, their finely tuned capacity to take umbrage and their list of off-territory topics, they were welcoming and convivial. They were tolerant of my occasional sermons even when I strayed into complex theology, and surprisingly comfortable with my received English accent when it came to readings and prayers.

There was no doubt, too, that they saw Sam and me as a couple with a gifted ministry. Previously, such a perception, prevalent as it was, made me feel diminished. I had a ministry of my own, and it irked that people saw me as co-reliant. I was also flattered when people at St Finnan's started turning to me for pastoral advice, something which had never happened in the past. It usually started with something like "What would you and Sam think…," which previously I would have found intensely patronising, but which now seemed curiously self-affirming given the obvious sincerity with which it was asked.

Naturally, I still met with Max on a monthly basis in respect of my ministerial ambitions. As soon as my new consultancy was up and running at a steady level – not so much as to pressure me, not so little as to risk fizzling out – I planned to start my training for ordination. But to be honest I was glad of the breathing space, and to be able to defer training for a year or even two. We had a steady string of visitors with really significant issues. People struggling with relationships, work situations, caring, teenage rebellion. All sorts of things that no-one looks to the church for guidance on any longer.

At first it irritated me. Why can't they sort these problems out for themselves or ask someone at the Council about them? If they must come to the church, why don't they ask Max or Ellie? Why do they want to pester people with work commitments? Gradually I started to realise it was precisely because we had work commitments, and shared the same daily pressures as they did, that they chose to speak to us. They didn't perceive us as being 'other-worldly'. These people let us into their dark places because they yearned for spiritual guidance on issues that really mattered to them. It struck me between the eyes one day when our neighbour Rachel confided in me, "You know, the church has been about as much use as a handbrake on a canoe before, but you're a breath of fresh air."

I've learned a lot about people since moving to Kilfinan, and I've learned a lot about myself. I didn't think I'd much more to learn when we left Lincolnshire; I'd got lots of life experience and had found my still point in the turning world, as Eliot put it. I was running headlong into a self-made future, when what I needed was to stand back and look at things from the perspective of eternity.

I don't know whether it's that the people here are different or that it's me who's changed; people are the same the world over, so I suspect the latter. Take Archie. He gave me the creeps at first, but now I've got to know him, we have a good laugh together. Take Karen. Nutty as a fruitcake but wise as Solomon in a crazy sort of way. And take Max. Almost as much a middle-of-the-road makeweight as Sam, or at least that was my initial impression. Until he gave me space to discover my real self. I can see now how he guided me into new places, continually nudging me outside my comfort zone, gently making me confront situations I'd been avoiding.

And then there's Ellie. Good old Ellie. No-one seems to notice her, but she's a brick. I pitied her at first – poor little widow with a narrow and lonely life. But get to know her and she's sharp as a tack, misses nothing. Never a bad word to say about anyone, but a fount of home truths that they'd probably sooner not hear. After really getting to know her, I opened up and asked her to be honest about me. "I'm from Lincolnshire," I told her, "so you can be as blunt as you like."

"Penny, dear," she said, "I think you're wonderful, and the whole church treasures you more than you think. But you mustn't just pray for God's blessing on your plans. You must pray for God to bless you with His own plans. Think about it. Pray about it."

You might think it sounds friendly enough, but to be honest I was deeply hurt. It was a sort of bluntness I didn't expect and it cut deeper than she realised; or perhaps she realised exactly how deep it would cut, but said it anyway. And, of course, without intending the slightest malice, she'd put her finger right on my rawest nerve.

I was so affronted that I instinctively retorted, "Ellie, don't you try to control me."

My tone was so reproachful that I shocked myself.

But Ellie simply smiled generously. "And don't you try to control God, Penny," she replied so disarmingly that all I could do was smile in return.

And when I prayed about it, God said to me, in a voice I've never heard so plainly in my life, "Love them to bits." From then, I used prayer as a first, not a last, resort.

And the next time I saw Max, he pressed into my hand a leaflet about a short course in Christian counselling. He suggested it might interest me and, if it did, he was sure the church would cover the cost. It didn't immediately appeal – too touchy-feely by half

– but I couldn't find any peace until I finally agreed. Of course, money wasn't an issue and I would pay my own fees.

So here I am, able to offer counsel on a slightly more qualified and competent basis, rather than floundering amateurishly out of my depth. I'm beginning to reach far more people on the margins of the church than ever would have happened through just officiating at services. I'm using my marketing and organisational skills to help promote our Churches Together group and mobilise our carers' support network. Fortunately, I've had many years experience in delegating, so that something which might have burgeoned into a full-time job for many people has been compartmentalised into one day a week for me.

To cut to the chase, I temporarily shelved my plans for ministerial training in order to give myself space to pray through the alternatives. I thought that Max and Ellie would rejoice over this decision, which indeed they did in a cautious sort of way. But they both, independently of each other, surprised me with reminders that time was no longer on my side if I wanted to get selected for training and progress through the echelons.

But then I think, I'm not that old really; I do have a period of grace before age becomes a barrier. I still think that training for the priesthood – and beyond – is the likely option. But if and when I do put myself forward, I may be a little older, but I shall most definitely be wiser.

15. SAM:

Full Circle

I knew more than Penny thought I knew. I realised she had been unsettled, frustrated. When she threatened to leave me that day back in the summer of 2013, after I broke the news about taking a new job, it scarcely surprised me. Whilst I didn't like the idea of a separation, I'm ashamed to admit that I didn't dislike it as badly as I should have done.

She wasn't the only one in a rut. Colleagues and superiors might, in jest, refer to me as *Old Makeweight*, but it's said affectionately. Everyone was aware that I was a crafty beggar who got results and deserved a significant promotion.

When the company offered me Director of Operations at the Kilfinan office, it wasn't what I was anticipating. My first reaction was that it was a banishment to the gulags. But the company was decentralising. Modern technologies allowed international business to be conducted from virtually any corner of the globe. There was a new wave of construction work associated with the North Sea. What some might mistakenly have perceived as booting me out of harm's way was in fact a manifest opportunity.

Accepting it would force issues domestically. Penny was smart – not quite as smart perhaps as she thought she was, but then I would say that, wouldn't I? In terms of an ordination candidate, she certainly checked all the boxes on the Church of England's ticklist. If she wanted to stay and carve out her own destiny, so be it. I'd have been sad but not distraught; there would have been a sense of failure but not a crushing one. At least, that was my first reaction.

And, to my shame, I have to admit that only far later did I even think about what my sudden departure might mean for St John's. Just after I'd finished my training and become a fully fledged lay reader wasn't the best moment to walk out on our desperately over-stretched ministry team.

Sadly, I admit that the last thing I did was pray. Literally. After discussing the job offer with our CEO. After breaking it to Penny and not speaking to each other for two days. After talking it over with colleagues. After almost casually mentioning it to the vicar as a done deal. Eventually I did place it before God and realised how back-to-front I'd done things. Yet, to cut a long story short and despite realising the oafishness of my ways, I did come away with a strong sense of affirmation from on high.

Kilfinan it was to be. The deanery clergy and my fellow lay reader appeared visibly upset, even betrayed, but in the end they were persuaded that God was calling me to pastures new. At work, the initial jests had yielded to reassurances that this was a key post at a critical stage in the firm's re-structuring that needed to be placed in a safe pair of hands. Doubtless an extremely astute career move. Several colleagues confided that they envied me moving to such a scenic part of the world where quality of life was as high as property prices were low.

Penny accused me of gross selfishness and I thought she was going to leave on the spot, and I alarmed myself by my bluntly matter-of-fact reaction. As a matter of courtesy, I informed the children who, quite independently of each other, expressed surprise that we'd managed to live in Lincolnshire so long without going stir crazy and conceded that they might continue to visit us, even if it risked falling off the edge of the world.

After formally accepting the post things happened so quickly that I hardly had time to think about the fall-out. So it was a surprise to me when Penny breezed down a couple of mornings later and said, "Sorry about what I said the other day. Of course I'm coming with you. I've handed in my notice. I'm going to go freelance and make a fist of it in Kilfinan."

I'm not normally an emotional type and I didn't anticipate my reaction. Suffice to say that we hugged each other for so long that it nearly made me late for work.

The move took ten weeks but it seemed like as many hours. Within no time I had orchestrated a handover to my successor, met with my prospective management team, arranged for the company to buy our home and seen our belongings crated up. It seemed quite unreal when, one midsummer morning, we were starting the long trek north for an empty-nester life in an unfamiliar culture.

The first morning in our new house Penny shook me out of my slumbers to see the dawn. I feigned pleasure at the sight of shafts of light shimmering across the cerulean sky and sea, but would have preferred an extra half hour in bed. An hour later I kissed her farewell and headed to the office, leaving her to deal with a variety of local tradesmen to get the house in working order and set up a home office. We had failed to realise that, in this part of the world, *mañana* conveys rather too strong a sense of urgency.

I was so absorbed in, and taken up by the pace of, my initial days at work that I quite forgot to introduce myself to the local clergy; indeed, I'd scarcely managed to get into a routine of daily quiet times. However, we had discovered the website of a local Episcopal church called St Finnan's which conducted a 10.30 service. On our first Sunday morning we headed out, with a deep sense of unpreparedness combined with guilt at not already having met with the Rector and offered our services.

If we'd been ordinary incomers, I suppose we'd have shopped around for a church which best suited our needs and tastes. There was the Church of Scotland, which I'd heard had a rather sermonising style of worship, something not greatly to my liking. Then there was its far smaller sister church on the other side of town, struggling to reinvent itself and survive. There was a flourishing evangelical church with a rather ragtag congregation and an admirable commitment to social outreach; a loyal if ageing

Catholic church; a tiny time-capsule of a Baptist church; and the Episcopals. These traits I fathomed later, but they were unknown to me as we headed, out of a sense of obligation, to St Finnan's that first weekend.

The church proved to be simultaneously similar and different. The exterior and internal layout were familiar. The quantity and quality of stained glass windows, and saints they depicted, were familiar. The congregation was neither worryingly small nor surprisingly large, and its demographic neither frighteningly old nor excitingly young. The prayer book, whilst wrong-footing us at times, must have shared four-fifths of our accustomed liturgy. The congregation were mainly friendly and there was no outright coldness. There was a demure and dutiful lay reader called Ellie. The rector, who introduced himself as Max Maxwell, was on the ball. He asked all the right questions but was clearly caught off balance when we summarised our background. We quickly reassured him that we'd be happy to leave any further discussion until later in the week, whereupon he invited us round for a chat on Tuesday evening.

Our visit to the Rectory was most encouraging. Max produced an excellent coffee and slices of a hitherto unknown but delicious type of cake as we gradually progressed through the conversational ice-breakers to a more serious discussion of our possible contribution to the life and work of St Finnan's. As Max listened to me he slowly stopped responding with the textbook oral and visual signals of a trained listener, and began to fix us with silent incredulity.

Penny sensed it would be judicious for me to stop talking and nudged me accordingly.

Still stunned into silence, Max produced a handful of church magazines from the coffee table. He opened the March edition at the prayer page and pointed to his entry which read, "Please pray for Max and Ellie, that they may have additional ministry support as they endeavour to meet the spiritual and pastoral needs of our three churches."

He then turned to the corresponding page in April's issue, "Please continue to pray for Max and Ellie that God sends them assistance." He turned to the issues for May, June and July and showed us similar, increasingly urgent entreaties. And now it was August. He said that if I wished, he could arrange a full workload for me as of tomorrow, but I asked if I might be afforded 'light duties' in the first instance. He was equally interested in Penny's aspirations and assured her that the ministerial training available in Scotland was every bit as good as she would have received 'down south'. Discernment of a calling to ordination, he said, normally took quite a while but he was confident she could be fast tracked and suggested that she immerse herself in a specific church role in the interim.

She was encouraged by the warmth of reception and confessed to me later that she preferred her chances of a meteoric rise through the Scottish Episcopal church's relatively small and lean organisation. Max, by now, was on a roll and quickly noted that there was a vacancy for a prayer secretary, at least for a year so that the present incumbent could take a

sabbatical. In truth, Penny had never been a particularly prayerful or contemplative person. She hadn't
neglected prayer – well, not habitually at least – but
she treated it in a rather stiff and formal way, and
was ill-at-ease in small group situations. She didn't
jump at the offer but, seeing Max's face take on the
aura of a crestfallen spaniel, promised to give it due
consideration.

We returned home to peruse the sample of church
magazines and minutes of meetings which Max had
thrust into our hands. We may have been at the other
end of the country, but there was an instant familiarity
about the medium-sized congregation in an average
provincial town, stretched beyond its means and
trying to reinvent itself. It was far too early to form
an opinion of St Finnan's, or of Max and Ellie, but our
mutual reaction was one of cautious optimism.

In the next few weeks Penny agreed to become
interim prayer secretary. I've rarely seen her so
insecure about anything, but she felt it was a bridge
she would have to cross *en route* to ordination.
Indeed, it had been an extremely astute suggestion,
and this single act made me wonder whether behind
Max's anodyne mask might lurk a perceptive intellect.

Indeed, what I did come to see in Max during the
following months was an excellent judge of character
and situations. Without ever cajoling or manipulating, he carefully nudged us into new and sometimes
unexpected roles. And there was something, too,
about our vestry meetings – the way they somehow

struck a fine balance between amicability and argument, between digression and conclusiveness.

Penny had said my face looked a picture at our first vestry meeting. Beforehand, I'd groaned that the membership would comprise "the usual bunch of loopy idealists, uptight moralisers, community worthies, lost souls and acquiescent pewfodder".

"Don't be so testy", she chided. "The last thing we need is for you to be in one of your supercilious moods".

"Don't I just love these meetings", I continued laconically. "Three hours of opinionated natter leading to a load of impractical ideas that never get actioned".

According to Penny, my irritability had been apparent all evening, though I thought I'd behaved pretty well. But it was only during our second meeting that I began to appreciate something rather special happening. Somehow, these mildly ill-tempered gatherings were having their acrimonious edges planed off them, they were bringing out people's virtues, sticking to an agenda and leading to useful outcomes. Over the years they had landed people in roles which released their latent talents, re-invigorated liturgies and worship, re-ordered the church buildings, promoted youth work and discipleship, valued the wisdom of the elderly and served the community.

Of course, none of these can be achieved by human action alone, but neither can they be left solely to divine providence. Individuals make the difference, and I increasingly came to realise that, here, Max was the common denominator.

My growing admiration for Max's abilities led me to take on an unexpectedly substantial role, even officiating alone at the outlying churches and venturing deep into pastoral issues. Max seemed indecently excited by my business credentials and how these might help reach people, including the unchurched and dechurched, in weekday situations.

Much as I felt flattered by his over-estimation of my talents, I found myself quite unprepared for the sheer volume and diversity of problems that folk land at the feet of the clergy. I had hoped that Max might have mentored me more closely on such matters, but he took the principle of 'light touch' to a fault. I somewhat resented the patient guidance he gave to Penny in the cause of ensuring that the bishop would be impressed by her state of preparedness for 'discernment', the necessary prelude to ordination training.

"Look, Max", I had said to him eventually. "Of course I'm more than delighted to beaver away for St Finnan's. But at times it feels as if I'm doing two full-time jobs at once. "

"Yes, I realise we're asking rather a lot of you", he replied quickly but sympathetically. "I don't know how we'd be coping with all our activities if you hadn't arrived when you did." And the way in which he chose and articulated his words reminded me how fortunate we were to have a church which was indeed full of activity. I was lucky to be needed so badly.

"How have you settled in at your new job?", he continued.

"Well I'm getting up to speed, but I'm still on a steep learning curve. There's literally no end to the amount I should be doing. And I don't know if you're aware", I added hesitantly, "and please don't spread it around, but our marriage went through a very bad patch before we moved here. I need to spend more time with Penny, not less."

Max thought carefully, but once more replied with unexpected speed and firmness.

"Sam, I'm sorry if this sounds preachy, but you've got to put down some boundaries. Especially at work. It's even worse when you're a minister; you're in demand 24/7, which is something I'm going into with Penny at the moment. You have to set your own limits, prayerfully of course, or other people will try and set them for you."

I protested that this simply wasn't possible in my current work situation; he didn't appreciate the demands that were placed on me. But, actually, he did, and he offered some very practical suggestions.

In the weeks which followed I forced myself to exercise a new intensity of discipline to ensure that my evenings and weekends remained sacrosanct from work pressures. Quite unexpectedly, this resulted in my entire office being aware of my parallel life. I used my commitments at St Finnan's to lay down boundaries, and it became clear to colleagues that church life was every bit as important to me as monthly performance targets. It brought me a degree of respect that I hadn't anticipated – and, I

FULL CIRCLE

should add, a stimulus for colleagues to share confidences in quite unexpected ways. It is surprising how often unchurched people will seek spiritual advice when a private and confidential opportunity presents itself.

And I found, too, that our various pastoral activities were drawing Penny and I closer together. We were encountering a common endeavour in the tortuous issues of this microcosm of humanity.

I saw how Penny was starting to question her headlong rush towards ordination, spending more time in personal and group prayer and taking a deepening interest in the lives and loves of our variegated flock. She has always been perceived, both by herself and others, as intellectual rather than empathic – a mercurial thinker rather than a self-effacing people-person. Yet she began to flourish in her unanticipated role as *anam cara*, a confidential soulmate to several of our fellow travellers. Her ministry has been spectacular at a one-to-one level and she has used her new-found counselling talents to great effect. She has already helped to transform the lives of a number of people and, in so doing, sacrificed much of her personal ambition. Of course, I sensed that this might merely be a hiatus before moving forward to ordination, but she would be a better priest and – who knows? – maybe bishop, in the long run.

Thus it was that, by the end of our first year at Kilfinan, we found that this cosy little church in this unremarkable town had taken us completely away from our comfort zone. In our previous life, we had been secure in our perceptions of our spiritual gifts and callings. We had retained control over the compartmentalisation of our working and spiritual lives. I realise now that Max had been watching us, spiritually and gently, winkling out bits of information, discerning our particular gifts, suggesting ways we might help to connect with the difficult-to-reach crevices of the community. There's little doubt that we have been humbled a little, before being used to greater effect.

Yet for all his gravitas, Max had a whimsical, even mischievous side. Thus it was that, one balmy evening, I was full of curiosity as I headed to an extraordinary vestry meeting that Max had called. He had been rather mysterious about it, and I thought he seemed uncharacteristically fidgety as he drew the meeting to order.

"Well, thank you all for coming", he started. He paused and gnawed at his lower lip. "I know you are wondering what this is all about, so I'll cut to the chase. The fact is that I shall be leaving St Finnan's after the summer to take up an appointment at a college in Wales".

The collective gasp was followed by a stunned silence as we exchanged disbelieving glances. I felt as if I had been kicked in the midriff. After my initial, visceral reaction I was quickly overwhelmed by such an oppressive sense of betrayal that I could barely take in the remainder of his presentation or contribute to the following discussion. As if in a trance I heard him say that he had accepted a lectureship, that he felt he had taken his parish ministry as far as he could, and he feared that both he and the church would stagnate if he remained. It seemed impossible. I thought Max was like Beinn Bhreac, granitic and immovable.

I forced myself to be civil at the end of the meeting but stayed on for as little time as possible. On my return home, I'm afraid I rather intemperately let off steam at Penny. She bore my invective stoically, and appeared to share my anger at the inevitable responsibilities that would fall on me. I railed at Max's selfishness – such things don't just happen overnight, and surely he had been plotting his departure for months! He was taking advantage of 'Old Makeweight', the sap who had arrived at just the right time for him to make his exit. A chance to offload burdens onto a trusty workhorse and save an over-stretched church a few bob by getting amateurs to carry the can. I took Penny's near silence as agreement.

Worse still, it was my turn to preach on Sunday, and I found myself quite unable to draft a gracious and upbeat sermon. I stared at the Lectionary readings blankly and, however sincerely I tried, could only see righteous anger and indignation staring back at me. The only slightly hopeful reading was from Psalm 37, which is not my favourite scripture at the best of times. I have more difficulty than most in sharing David's optimism that justice will triumph over evil, especially when I watch the daily news. Try as I might, I found myself only able to use the Psalm as ammunition against Max – that, in his self-centred personal ambitions, he might wither like the grass or vanish like smoke.

Fortunately, Penny retrieved the situation with a last ditch suggestion that she do the sermon in my stead. She didn't relish the prospect but had a new and as yet unannounced reason to grasp this particular thistle – she had recently been approved for ordination training. It was exactly the sort of tricky situation that might test her mettle.

By Sunday morning I was feeling slightly more even-tempered and was rather mischievously looking forward to seeing how the congregation would react to Max's announcement. In the event, I wasn't disappointed by their air of alarm and disappointment. He had set so many hares running in recent years that there was bound to be dismay about him choosing to leave us at this juncture.

With a deafening silence of disbelief around us, I whispered "Follow that!" in Penny's ear. But her sanguine nod conveyed that she was, indeed, about to do so with aplomb.

I settled back in my seat as she briefly composed herself at the lectern.

"It's all about timing, isn't it? Our choices and decisions in life are, of course, important in themselves. But their timing can be equally important. It's not just a matter of what we decide to do: it's also a matter of knowing when to do it, when to announce it, and when to discuss it with others."

"Not a bad start under the circumstances", I mused.

"In Psalm 37, David was facing difficult choices. He had many opponents. Indeed, they seemed to be flourishing whilst he appeared to be failing. But

David knew it was an illusion – just a temporary situation. So he wrote, 'Commit your way to the Lord…trust in Him…be still before the Lord and wait patiently for Him'. If David was to succeed he would have to be patient. He would not only need to choose God's way, but also patiently await God's perfect timing. Max has told us today of his brave decision; and I'm sure he feels that not only is the way right, but also the timing is perfect."

By now, Penny had aroused my curiosity. It was an impeccable start, and I hoped she might be going to suggest that Max was deceiving himself about hearing God's call. But I was brought sharply to my senses when I heard her say, "I remember when we announced our departure at St John's, how some of our friends felt a sense of betrayal, as if this was the worst possible moment for us to be moving on."

Suddenly, I wasn't sure that I liked where the sermon was going. At least she might have asked me before dredging up the past. It took me a moment to re-focus on what she was saying.

"How can we be sure that we've chosen the right path and the perfect timing?", I heard her say. "Well, of course, we can never be certain because we aren't God and we're living in an imperfect world. However, there are some things we can do as a matter of good practice. For example, no matter how busy we are, we must make time to pray and seek guidance from scripture."

I began to fidget uneasily. It was almost as if she was directing her comments at me rather than Max.

"And of course we need to discuss our intentions openly with those who are closest to us, even if this risks their opposition. It's probable – in fact I know for certain – that Max has prayed over this decision with his family, and they are now giving him their full support."

I felt my ears burn with almost painful intensity.

"And you have to be honest with yourself. You have to be gracious enough to ask God for a warning sign if something isn't the right choice. If we really, honestly entrust the matter to God, we'll receive all sorts of unexpected signals that this is either the wrong step at the wrong time or else the most inspired next action. Don't you find that? I know I always do. So I'm sure that over the past days, Max and his family will have been receiving all manner of little affirmations about the wisdom of their joint decision."

By this stage I was feeling so paranoid and distracted that I missed the end of the sermon, but I suspect it was rather good because the congregation seemed to be almost on the point of applause. And when Penny resumed her seat next to me her face conveyed the most inscrutable butter-wouldn't-melt-in-my-mouth expression. I patted her hand reassuringly about her performance, although I relied on autopilot to see me through the remainder of the service.

As I mentioned some time ago, Penny rarely comments on my sermons and on this occasion I returned the compliment. I cooked lunch in recognition that today she had been the 'worker', and afterwards steered our conversation towards safer topics.

In the ensuing days, of course, Ellie and I had detailed discussions with Max during which he reassured us about the professional cover we would receive. Following one meeting, Ellie noted my furrowed brow and chided me for my lack of faith. Hadn't she warned me, soon after my arrival, that Max was almost too good to be true? By which she meant, of course, that he was probably too good to last. Hadn't she counselled me not to over-depend on him? Max had given us over a decade of fabulous service and no-one could ask for more.

I couldn't gainsay her prescience, but my mind was still exercised about the burden that would fall on me. Getting a series of retired and visiting priests for a couple of hours a week was different from having a gifted full-time incumbent of our own, and somehow Ellie and I would need to maintain the enthusiasm and vibrancy of St Finnan's over the other 166 hours in the week. Ellie would be doggedly loyal and dutiful, of course, but she was now quite elderly and I had to watch that she didn't over-extend herself.

I tried not to brood on the matter, but must have been repressing more anger than I realised. Finally, it all spilled over one evening when Ellie and I were shutting up shop following a Finance Committee. I'd been careful not to wash dirty linen in public, but when we were alone I suddenly burst into a tirade about how Max was manipulating me. I endeavoured to control my tongue, but left Ellie in no doubt about my strength of feeling.

She was clearly shocked. She hadn't seen me angry before, or openly critical of someone at church, least of all a person of authority.

"Sam, please don't talk about Max like that", she snapped defensively. "Max would never exploit anyone."

"Look, Ellie, I'm sorry. I don't want to upset you. It isn't your fault. But I don't believe that Max hasn't been plotting this for ages. He's using us – me in particular – as an escape route. Doesn't he care what sort of state St Finnan's gets into without a full-time minister?"

I forced myself to shut up so as not to cause further hurt; yet, even as I spoke, I could see in Ellie's face that she had found her still point. Her winsome smile foretold that that sage advice would shortly be forthcoming.

Begrudgingly, I muttered, "Okay than, convince me".

"Sam. This really was something that came up completely out of the blue, and Max agonised over it. It's been a difficult family decision but it's probably good timing in terms of the children's education. And I don't think he'd have agreed unless he had absolute confidence in you. Or in Penny and me."

It was typical of Ellie to place herself last.

"For a start", she continued, "he had become increasingly certain that God was calling him to do something new. You must have noticed how restless he'd become after your arrival. How, he envied your ability to connect with people in their daily situations. Not that he had much time to brood over it, of course. He felt he'd given St Finnan's everything he could and it was time for a new ministry. The details and timing were unclear but he was prepared to move to wherever and whatever he was being called. And out of the blue he was asked by an old friend to apply for the College post. He hadn't even seen the advert. I'm sure that a lot of prayer went into it. I know his family have spent a long time discussing it."

"And what about us? Isn't he concerned about the gap he's leaving?"

"Well, think about it Sam. Has Max ever given you space to develop your preaching talents?"

"Yes, of course, but…"

"And has he led you and Penny into distinctive areas of ministry."

"Yes, but not always the ones we would have chosen…"

"Perfect", she smiled. " And aren't you beginning to be accepted as a local?"

"Well that would be putting it a bit too strongly…"

"Or gaining people's confidences, at least. Starting to become an insider. And haven't you got a foot in the door of local schools and workplaces…"

"I suppose if you…"

"And what about him letting you chair church meetings and working groups. Nobody's better at conducting business than you…"

"Now you're just flattering me…"

"Not in the slightest. Hasn't Max just successfully arranged for Penny to start her ministerial training?"

"Yes, I suppose so." I paused.

"Sam, if there's ever such a thing as perfect timing, this is it. I know it'll be difficult for us, but hereabouts we have a proverb that 'God shapes the back for the burden'. We'll be given strength and help as we need it, and we'll all grow together."

"I wish I could believe you", I replied with slightly more resignation in my voice. "But how long might it be before we get a replacement? Going by recent experience it could be two or three years. I can't even contemplate the prospect."

And how quickly have the last two years gone?" she asked.

"Like a flash," I conceded.

"Well then," smiled Ellie, "I can assure you that, as you get older, time will seem to pass even quicker. Cheer up, Sam, there are angels out there who will come to our rescue. We won't recognise them, but they'll appear at just the right moments to nourish and sustain us. You just watch how St Finnan's will grow through this experience. I've seen it before. God will never let us down."

And do I believe she's right? Most definitely! These days I know for certain that we entertain angels unawares. There are some clear candidates. Lloyd would be my principal contender, but I suspect we've met several others in recent years. Perhaps I was speaking to one right there.

"Just think," added Ellie as we were tidying up. "In three years time Penny will be a curate. Perhaps she's our future priest!"

And, noticing I'd been stunned into silence, she added, "I'll set the alarm and lock up, Sam. You pop off home."